The Dark Era

By: James Eddy

[978-0-9930732-2-9]

TABLE OF CONTENTS

PUBLISHERS NOTES

For information contact; http://www.jameseddy.co.uk

Book and Cover design by JLR Photography and Lauren Bathurst
Used under a Standard Royalty-Free License.

ISBN: 978-0-9930732-2-9

Print Edition

First Published 2014 by Youngblood Books

James Eddy

DEDICATION

This book is dedicated to: All of the Eddys, Sajdoks and their many offshoots around the world.

Love to all my family and friends.

PART 1

'May your strength give us strength
May your faith give us faith
May your hope give us hope
May your love give us love'.

"Into the Fire"
Bruce Springsteen

CHAPTER 1

Karski opened his eyes and tried to breathe. He couldn't. Something was blocking his throat and nostrils. Fighting for breath, he felt his heart beating. His limbs flailed. Ineffective. Useless. He surrendered to it and drank it down. Slowly allowing himself to become one being and one essence. And all of it was liquid and choking darkness and then it was nothing at all. Fear grew within his chest and the world seemed to slip away.

Karski saw glittering shades of blue, purple, yellow, and orange within the clear liquid, which was also the closest thing to air in this place. The ripples of coloured light and warm bubbles of luminescence were the imperfections in something that was absorbing and being absorbed by his body.

And in an instant it was all over and he was plunging beneath the surface of a liquid that was much more familiar. The water was freezing but he hardly felt it at all. His earlier struggle had already weakened his body, if not his spirit. He was exhausted and drowning again until two hands grabbed his arms and pulled him up onto a river bank.

He was barely conscious but, as the light gradually returned to his eyes, his mind went somewhere else entirely. Images went flashing through it like a parade of horror emanating from the future and the past at the same time. He was shown a great city in ruins; a blonde woman in a red dress; exterminating angels with black wings and eyes filled with flames; and three sad indentations in three empty mattresses. He didn't recognise or understand any of what he saw.

"Are you all right, friend?" he heard someone say.

The voice cut through the disorder and brought his mind back. By then, the water had been absorbed by his skin and he got to his feet feeling nothing. There was no cold, no warmth, no pains, cuts or bruises. Only emptiness remained.

"Yes I think so," he replied, without looking at the man who had just saved him.

Instead, he looked everywhere else. The most noticeable thing then was that there seemed to be no sun in the sky. What remained was a low-powered light in the form of a misty blue haze that was coating the entire world around him. It was a haze that was only distorted by small ripples he saw every time he blinked his eyes.

It briefly looked like the only other source of light was the glistening silver lava shining on the snow covered ground and trees. Except that it only lasted until Karski blinked his eyes again. Just another distortion in what wasn't quite the air.

Suddenly, a bullet buzzed past his right ear and he instinctively threw himself onto the snow.

"GET UP QUICK!" the other man shouted, grabbing him roughly by the arm and dragging him onto his feet.

More bullets followed them as they ran into a more densely covered part of the forest they were in. As they ran deeper into it, vast oak trees towered above them; their trunks becoming embedded with ricocheting bullets as the two men passed; darting between them, looking for cover.

"This way," the man said, turning towards an even thicker line of trees and emerald undergrowth.

Karski followed without question. As he ran, he picked up his knees to avoid being tripped by the longer grass on the ground. He quickly looked back to check on their pursuer and only saw trees and greenery.

"Here," the man said sharply, causing Karski to look at him directly for the first time.

All that he saw was the fear in the man's darkened eyes. It was a look he understood and it was enough to concentrate his mind in the moments that followed.

"Stand completely still and try not to struggle," the man told him.

"What?"

The question was unnecessary. Karski was already sinking. The ground rapidly reached his ankles and then his knees. The feeling of pinpricks travelling and numbing their way up his body went with it. He looked over to the man who had put him into this situation and saw that he was also sinking.

Both of them were soon covered all the way up to their shoulders. The man looked at Karski again and told him, "Try to stay as still as possible and just breathe... Be calm."

There was no time for any other words before the ground covered both his mouth and Karski's ears. Everything was silent. Karski's breathing remained normal, his heart rate was steady, and he did exactly what he had been told. He kept his eyes open to peer through the grey earth at the vast network of roots from trees and grass, that delved deep down, perhaps even to the core of the world.

He looked at the other man and found he wasn't looking back at him. Instead, he was staring up at the surface of the ground, at a winged creature, as big as a man, which had just landed on it. Karski followed his eye line. The creature had its back to him and he watched as its wings folded down. Not covered in feathers, these wings had a harsher simplicity to them; more like the wings of a bat, black leather, stretched and taut over muscle. They had a raw power that made him feel truly afraid.

Its short legs were completely covered in light brown hair and it had hooves that stepped rather uneasily over the ground through the long grass. It was only when it turned around that Karski got to see its full fearsomeness. The combination of a pale human torso, powerful arms, blonde hair, and horns protruding from just above its temples were undoubtedly a fearsome sight. But it was the flames and deadness within its eyes that scared him most. At that moment, Karski believed it was a creature which was almost unstoppable.

His breathing quickened and so did the blinking of his eyes, although he didn't shift from where he was until long after the grotesque soldier had opened its wings and flown away. When he turned his head to look at the other man again, he found that half of his body was already above the surface.

Karski lifted an arm and slowly rose up out of the ground; pushed upwards by unseen hands. The hand of the other man reached down to take hold of his and helped speed up the process.

"We should be safe for now," he told Karski, once they were standing on the ground again.

He smiled and Karski finally managed to look at him a little more closely. He was a tall man with broad shoulders and short dark hair, receding a little at the temples. His eyes were deep set and he had a thick protruding nose. The odd thing to Karski was that, while he was dressed smartly in neutral colours, his appearance managed to be both memorable and forgettable at the same time.

He gave the impression of being a man who walked without any kind of fear. He certainly seemed to know exactly where he had to go, and where he needed to be. And without question, Karski followed him through the thickest, darkest area of trees, where there appeared to be almost no light at all. He wasn't afraid, although he would have liked to know what was going on or at least where it was they were heading. It made no difference and the other man made no attempt to stop and explain.

Karski decided not to argue. There wasn't much choice. He had no idea where he was, so he could hardly travel alone. It seemed more sensible to wait. They had to stop at some point and when they did he could ask all the questions he wanted.

They went on in virtual silence. The only sound being their shoes stepping over the long grass. That swiftly turned into steps on earthy ground and then into the crunch of snow as the two men reached another icy clearing.

Pale nothingness was all around them and for the first time Karski was able to see the mountains that surrounded the forest on three of its sides. He immediately understood that these were the cause of the forest's permanent misty vagueness.

"We should rest here," the man told him.

Karski wasn't tired but didn't disagree. He decided not to sit down on the soft snow. Instead, he walked towards a vast lake that was half lost in the fog. He strained his eyes and was able to see the effects that the stillness and cold had upon its surface. Ice had formed into wafer thin islands broken up by the little remaining heat of the still water surrounding them. Karski couldn't help gazing at them with a strange sense that these islands were waiting for something; for warmth or the sun to return, and only so they could finally be allowed to disappear.

He walked to the edge of the lake for a closer look and found that the water there wasn't as icy. He looked down and caught a glimpse of his reflection. It was enough to send shockwaves racing through him, from his mind, and into every single muscle and fibre of his body. He turned his eyes away and then back again but what he saw didn't change.

It wasn't horror or even fear that he felt at that moment. It was simply that the face looking back at him wasn't a face that he remembered.

CHAPTER 2

Short, dark blonde hair and pale blue eyes peered a little too long at their own reflective glory. He straightened his tie and looked at the small amount of grey in his hair. A sigh escaped his lips.

David Gombrowicz couldn't even try to pretend that the beauty of his youth wasn't very much in the past. He ran his right hand through his hair and left the bathroom. Everything was quiet as he went into the bedroom. That wasn't unusual. Even after five years, his flat was still an empty, soulless space that had never felt like home. Picking up his shiny black leather briefcase, he walked to the front door; mentally running through everything he had to do that day, as he locked it behind him and walked to his car.

He was travelling to the train station, which was just across the river from where he lived. He always drove even though he could quite easily have got a bus or taxi. The reason for that was simple enough and David understood the irony in feeling safest in a car; cocooned from any unwanted noise or silence.

He opened the door and got inside, not noticing the May sunshine and fresh early summer air. After only a few deep breaths he felt completely calm. Turning the key in the ignition brought the engine to life and barely a second later the CD player started and drowned out the car's impressive growls.

Normally, he listened to *Born to Run* in the car. That day was different though, and he switched off 'Thunder Road' before it had a chance to truly get his blood pumping. He didn't normally watch or listen to the news in the morning but this was different. It was the day after a General Election that had no winner and that seemed important enough to make him want to hear about it.

He swiftly discovered that on Radio Four there was an awful lot of talk without many conclusions; just distracting and possibly inspired guesswork designed to deal with what was pretty much uncharted territory. All that anyone was able to declare with any certainty was that a Hung Parliament was unavoidable.

It didn't take long for David to question the sense in him listening. He was self-aware enough to realise that he was too old to listen too closely to anything that challenged his political opinions. It was far better, and simpler, for his thoughts to be confirmed, no matter what the strengths and weaknesses of the arguments. And as a result, the only thing these programmes ever did was make him angry and annoyed.

It was a mentality that had come to reflect his voting habits over the years. He was a Labour man and always had been. Every few years he would go and put a cross next to their box, no matter how detached and disaffected he might have become with the party. It was just something he did and he didn't really know why anymore. He'd always told himself that he simply couldn't vote for anyone else and, by then, that had become the truth.

He was the son of an immigrant, brought up in a poor neighbourhood. He thought that had to count for something. But there was something else at stake. David had an unshakeable need to believe that the party were like him. That they might both have been compromised in a lot of ways, but, in principle, they were still the same as they'd always been.

On that day though, he couldn't help wondering if he was just lying to himself; perhaps the act of voting was all that was left of the person he'd once been. He certainly couldn't deny that the distance from his past and even to his family had grown horribly wide during the comfortable course of his life.

He sighed again, and switched off the radio. Already at the station, he took his briefcase, locked the car, and walked inside the darkened glass terminal. With ticket in hand, David went through the barriers without any difficulty. He was a little bit early and so he went and bought a newspaper, sat down on one of the benches, and waited.

His confusing array of thoughts turned to Charlie Mejdek; another Polish immigrant's, son. He was thirty years younger than David and he was about to go to prison for at least six months. David was the man defending him in court and he increasingly found the entire case utterly depressing, not least because he knew that Charlie was an innocent man.

It appeared to be a simple breaking and entering case with no witnesses and very little material evidence linking anyone directly to the crime. This should have meant Charlie was completely above suspicion. And then everything changed due to one key piece of evidence: Ten days after the crime was reported Charlie had walked into Alveston police station and admitted to everything.

Until that moment, he hadn't even been considered a suspect and there was something about that which didn't feel quite right to David. That feeling only grew when he found out that the police's main suspect had previously been a young man named Peter Gillespie.

Gillespie was a nobody, in general terms. However, he was known to be an associate of Lucien Costello; a powerful businessman who had once had links with the Richardson family in London, before moving away and striking out on his own; perhaps more importantly though, Peter Gillespie was also Charlie Mejdek's best friend.

When Mejdek confessed, all the enquiries into Gillespie were immediately dropped. David had suspected that some pressure may have been placed on the police to simply make do with putting Charlie away. That only confused him more because he couldn't work out why anyone would go to so much trouble to keep someone as insignificant as Gillespie out of prison. There was something he was missing in all of this and it troubled him a great deal.

David was aware that it wasn't sensible to look at things in such an emotionally irrational way. The law was always paramount in any kind of criminal case, but he liked Mejdek. He was a nice boy and David suspected that all he was trying to do was keep his best friend out of prison and out of trouble. Of course, that didn't make what he was doing any less foolish or naïve. And that was another thing he couldn't understand because he really didn't think that Charlie was either of those things.

The train arrived, a little bit late, and David got on. Once he found his seat he sat down and looked at the newspaper. It was just more election stuff, already outdated by the events of the last twenty-four hours. He briefly flicked through the sports pages before laying the paper down on the table in front of him.

One of his main reasons for commuting by train was that the journey was a little over an hour, which usually gave him just enough time to catch up on some paperwork before getting into London. He briefly considered reading some of his work papers but he wasn't really in the mood that morning and there wasn't anything he particularly needed to do anyway.

Leaning back in his seat, he looked out of the window instead. Staring into the distance, where the miles seemed to roll by at a much more luxurious pace, he noticed the huge metallic towers that joined up the powerlines. His son, Jonathon, had used to say they were the skeletons of giant robots from an earlier, grander civilization. He'd only been a little boy then but he'd always had a wild imagination. David smiled for a moment.

Then his smile evaporated as he immediately understood why he was so concerned about Charlie. He'd seen plenty of cases and circumstances that were similar to this one. However, there was a key difference. Somewhere during the course of it, David's concern for Mejdek had become almost parental. He was feeling less like a Barrister and a lot more like a worried parent dealing with a wayward son. It was a feeling David was very familiar with. And on top of that, Charlie and Jonathon were more or less the same age.

These were not thoughts or feelings that David could air publically but he was increasingly aware that he'd never been hard-nosed enough to be the massively successful lawyer he might once have become. Even for someone working in Legal Aid he had too much empathy, while his stunning inability to hide it did him no favours either.

Morality and legality weren't always the same thing and that troubled him more with each passing year. In some ways, the Charlie Mejdek case was just another example of his weakness; his professional Achilles heel, although it really changed nothing. He could only believe what he believed and he couldn't help thinking that while Charlie may not have been doing the legally correct thing, he was actually doing something completely understandable and, perhaps even, right.

All that left him with was the hope that Peter Gillespie, and whoever else was involved, in whatever was going on, appreciated what Charlie was doing for them. David remained just cynical enough to assume that they didn't.

The last time he'd seen Charlie, had been after the legal formality of the Arraignment hearing into the burglary. There had been nothing he could do to change the outcome of that. A guilty plea had been entered and little else. Afterwards though, he and Charlie had spoken about what would happen after sentencing and Mejdek had been completely honest with him for the first time. Mostly, he'd talked about staying out of trouble and living quietly in Alveston when he got out. Then he'd looked David directly in the eyes.

"I didn't rob that house ya know," he'd said, "But I'll still do whatever I have to do."

David had thought about what to do with this information and quickly realised it wouldn't help. Presenting this evidence would only lead to a charge of perjury and wasting police time and a much heavier prison sentence for Charlie. He knew it wasn't worth it. It still wouldn't be justice.

"I know," he'd told him and left it at that.

David got off the train at St Pancras and walked through the station to get on the tube. The Circle Line took him into central London. For most of his adult life he'd liked travelling on the underground. For some people it was too cramped and congested but when he was younger that was the part he'd liked most; the fact that they were all in it together. It wasn't quite the same anymore and he certainly felt more intimidated than he used to; although he could just as easily have said that about a lot of things. He wondered if it might have been down to his age.

When he got onto the Central Line, the train took him to Holborn station. He got out and walked along Kingsway to the legal chambers. He was ready. Prepared for the near impossible task of cutting Charlie Mejdek's prison sentence down to the barest minimum.

CHAPTER 3

We actually nicked the armchair from a skip outside someone's house. We were pissed but it wasn't really like a normal Thursday night. It was all Patrick's idea, so what could I do? The lesson I've learned is that if Patrick Anders ever tells you to do something, it's better, and easier, just to do it.

A few Saturday's before, we were both round at Bear's place drinking lager till about four in the morning. I don't remember why it was just us there but I sort of remember talking about buying a sofa just so we could ride it down Cuckoo Hill sometime.

We've all got previous for wasting money on stupid ideas so that was nothing new. But Bear got really excited about it and kept saying, "We really have to do this, boys, we really do."

So Patrick and me were both like, "Yeah, yeah, it's a great idea, mate." And then after we left there, I managed to forget all about it until Patrick brought it up again at The Bell that Thursday night.

Robbie Godwin and Dan were there when we arrived. It was half eight and I was pretty skint before we even started. But Patrick kept buying me drinks and then Allen turned up a bit later to throw his cash around and give us a few of his usual pearls of wisdom. I've got to say that I fucking love that guy. Never fails to keep me drinking, which is never a good idea but it's definitely fun while it lasts.

It soon kind of got out of hand and there was a hell of a lot of talking bollocks and laughing at each other. And in the middle of it all Patrick starts taking the piss out of this sofa thing Bear was going on about.

"What a stupid, fucking waste of money that'd be," he was bellowing through the alcoholic fumes, "He should put that money towards actually cleaning that fucking flat of his."

And we all laughed. And it's true but we won't tell Bear that, because we can't. None of us are brave enough to be better friends to him. Allen bought us all another couple of drinks and we all forgot about it again for a while.

My head was swimming by the time Dan suddenly remembered something:

"I think there's an armchair in a skip next door to my house".

There was hardly a pause.

"We're definitely having that," Patrick said, and I knew he wasn't kidding.

But that's when Bulmer came into the pub and invited us all back to his place for an after party. It was still only just a bit after ten, so we had a few more doubles before we piled outside and headed down the road; not remembering anything about Patrick's vaguely brilliant plan.

I say that it's Bulmer's place but that isn't totally true. It's actually his parent's house. But because they're always away he gets the run of the place. And so, obviously, we completely take advantage of that.

As we walked, I sent Cassidy a text to see if she fancied coming round. No reply though. I figured she was probably with the guy she'd been seeing. Best just to leave her alone although I wished I hadn't lost her brother's number too. But then he was probably busy with Marie anyway.

It was certainly warm outside and we didn't have to walk far. Heading straight into the kitchen, Bulmer fixed me a drink, and then fucked off outside to get stoned.

I wandered through the converted barn looking for Patrick again. It wasn't difficult. Just follow the laughter. He'd gone back to yammering on about the armchair with Robbie and Dan. And between the three of them they'd managed to come up with the new and improved concept of '*Pimp My Armchair*'.

None of us were in a fit state to need much convincing to go rooting through a skip outside Dan's neighbour's house. And it was only once we were wandering along the road, that Robbie thought to ask, "Where are we gonna put this thing once we get it?"

It was a fair point. He had a car in his garage, me and Dan don't even have garages and Patrick lives three miles away, which was probably a bit too far to lug an armchair.

It didn't matter. We saw a shaved head shining in the street lights, moving towards us and we knew it was Dragon on his way to Bulmer's. We told him what we were doing and, as soon as we did, he wanted to help.

"Park it in front of my house till the morning. No-one's gonna be parking there anyway."

So, he went on to Bulmer's and we walked up the road to get our armchair. The closer we got, the harder we tried to be quiet and the more we laughed at what we were going to do. I tried to compose myself as we got to the skip but as soon as Patrick threw himself headfirst into it, I was laughing like an idiot again.

When I looked up, Robbie was in there with him and passing the chair down to me and Dan.

Then we legged it about a hundred yards down the road, stopped and put it down on the uneven tarmac.

"Let's try it out," Patrick said, sitting down in it.

So we pushed him along and then down the slight dip that was in the road. The shock is that he didn't actually fall out of it until the plastic wheels under the chair melted from the speed he was travelling at. He spilled out onto the road, a little grazed and bruised beneath blue jeans and sky blue jumper, and I knew he wouldn't feel a thing until morning at the earliest.

Obviously, the melted wheels made it a lot more difficult to push the armchair to Dragon's house and we ended up carrying it most of the way. Then we dumped it, slightly lopsided, against the kerb.

I was feeling knackered by then, so I headed home. Stumbling through the dark at half two in the morning, I could already tell it was going to be a long day.

CHAPTER 4

Short dark blonde hair and pale blue eyes were reflected back at him. This wasn't a surprise. It was the youthfulness of his other features that he found strange. He shook his head and looked over to the other man.

"Not what you expected?" he asked him, without looking up.

"No... I didn't really expect anything," said Karski.

"That's because you don't know where you are... In fact, you probably don't even know who you are."

"Yes, that's right."

"Then it's a good job I'm here to tell you. I know exactly where you are Mr Karski."

He searched through what little memory he had and found that the name still meant nothing to him. The other man simply sat and waited until he walked slowly towards him and sat on the soft snow a few feet away. It was only then that he started to tell Karski his story. It didn't begin well:

"The truth is that you are in pretty much the worst place in the entire world and you are here at just about the worst time ever... This place is the Tarek Nor forest in Pileck, and there is a war that is taking place all around us. We are not the cause of it but we have been placed at the centre of it. There is no way out for us without fighting."

He took a deep breath as Karski tried to take in exactly what he was being told.

"The creature you saw was a Sinistrian and there are literally millions more like him flying over Pileck and killing any of us they can find. They are very dangerous creatures, and that would be bad enough, but there are other dangers to our people…

"Dangers?"

"There are also the Curzonians… They have an empire about the same size as the Sinistrian's and for years they've both used us as a buffer between them. They are meant to be our allies but I know they cannot be trusted… All they are really doing is waiting while innocent Pilecki blood is spilled, so that when we're at our weakest, they can move in and take what's ours for themselves."

Karski thought he understood. There was something familiar about what the man was saying.

"And how exactly do you know all this?" he asked him.

"I'm a courier. I have to carry information between us and our true friends in this war," the man explained, "It takes me over and around all the areas under Sinistrian control, so it's hardly the safest job in the world. But then, no job's very safe right now and it's something that has to be done… Information is the key to our survival and we have to stay in contact the outside world, no matter what it takes."

With each word, Karski's admiration for the man's bravery grew.

"I would rather die than do nothing and simply let the enemies of all the things that are good in this world carve up and destroy us. I will make any sacrifice necessary to make sure that doesn't ever happen."

There was silence and they both sat looking at each other until Karski eventually spoke again:

"Who are you?"

"You can call me Witold."

He nodded his head and asked him, "How did the war start?"

Witold didn't answer. Instead, he slowly got up onto his feet.

'I will tell you but now isn't the time…We need to get moving. It's not a good idea to stay in one place for too long, especially out in the open like this. I've got to deliver a report from my latest mission. It's a ten mile walk but it's mostly under the cover of the trees. It should be fairly safe as long as we don't run into a Sinistrian patrol."

He didn't say anything else and simply led the way out of the clearing and into the dense forest. Karski followed, quiet and compliant and it didn't take long for him to completely lose all concept of distance and time. He soon had little idea of how far the two of them had walked. It seemed to be much further than the ten miles Witold had suggested and he started to wonder how much further they could possibly have left to go. Then quite suddenly, the other man stopped and dropped down onto the grass. Almost as a reflex action, Karski did the same thing.

They both looked up through the trees and undergrowth. Six Sinistrians were rounding up at least twenty men, women, and children. Witold looked at Karski, who continued to watch as two Sinistrians led one of the men away from the main group.

"There's too many of them and they're too well armed. We can't help." Witold whispered.

The two Sinistrians stopped and stepped away from the man. Then, in full view of all the others, they opened fire on him with their machine guns. The man slumped to the ground and a woman screamed. The two Sinistrians immediately moved back to the group of Pilecki and grabbed the woman. She was to be next.

In that instant, the anger in Karski grew. He stood up. Witold tried to hold him back. He was too strong. Without another thought, he sprinted towards the two Sinistrians that were manhandling the woman and just as he reached them everything suddenly went dark.

CHAPTER 5

I'm woken by the sound of banging on the front door. It's ten past nine so I'm already running late. I'm completely fucking shattered. I get to the door, as quick as I can and see Stephen through the glass. I unlock and pull the door open to ask, "What do you want Nowak?"

He grins, which is sort of unusual for him.

"Just thought I'd stay here today. You mind?

He already knows that I don't. He spends most of his time here anyway.

"I've gotta go out in a bit but stick around as long as you want, mate."

He comes inside and heads into the living room as I go back to my room to get changed.

By the time I come out, he's already playing on the X-Box; the boy's bloody obsessed with '*Mass Effect*'.

"Dunno what time I'll be back but I'll see you later," I tell him.

He looks up and nods his head and then looks back at the screen. I don't bother locking the door behind me and walk quickly down the road. As I go past Dragon's house I see the armchair is gone and I wonder what the hell they did with it after I went to bed.

It's a warm morning, and the sun is out, but my eyes sting and I'm not feeling any less tired yet. Waiting for the bus is when the nerves start taking hold and then I'm struck by the realisation that I should've double checked that she was still coming today. It's not like she's always that reliable. Of course, I'm not either but that's hardly the point.

I'm tapping out a text to her but it's already too late. The bus has arrived, so I step inside and look towards the back. And she's there. She smiles and I do too.

I pay the driver and go to her.

"Hello, stranger," I say because I can't think of anything else and I'm too tired to recognise just how fucking lame that is.

"Hi."

She looks good and I've missed her. I've missed my friend. We both make sure not to mention anything about what happened. That way, there's no blame.

"Are you okay?" is all I ask.

And so I don't say anything about the fact we've hardly spoken since we broke up, even though we weren't even together that long. Or that there's no real excuse for that because I've tried and she knows I've tried. But then that just means it's down to her, I guess.

In all honesty, I think of precisely none of those things then. I just love seeing her and being around her. It's been like that since the first night we met.

We end up talking about nothing in particular and she makes me laugh. Bloody girl! She has an unparalleled ability to make everything in her life seem so dramatic.

"I've missed you," she tells me, and I believe her but only really because I want to.

Then she tells me all about her new job and how she's working in a Womenswear Department of a shop. She tells me about all the people who are lovely and all about the ones that look down on her for not wearing enough brand name clothes.

There seem to be more of the latter than the former and she talks about them for a while. But I know she doesn't really care all that much about those people. She's heading off somewhere that's way beyond them, and beyond their bitchiness. She doesn't even need to tell me that the job's just a means to an end for her. All the jobs she's ever had have just been a way to make money before she becomes an actress. And it's just another way to fill time to avoid overthinking her life.

The thing is I know that she's going to do it. Mary's just about the bravest of all the friends I have. She carries all these doubts around with her and I still know that she's going to be everything she can be. She's a shooting star and I'm not sure I can stop her leaving me behind or even that I should. And then I think she really will break my heart.

"Beach today then," I ask

"Yes, indeed my darling boy."

"You know this is just about the first time I've been to Yarmouth."

"Really?"

"Well, I did go to the Pleasure Beach for my eighteenth birthday and got my wallet nicked. And I decided then that I didn't really want to go back."

"Oh… Maybe it's not such a good idea then."

"No, it's all right. I didn't really think I had too much choice if I actually wanted to get to see you."

I know it's a cheap shot but it comes out of my mouth before I can stop it. Mary lowers her head and I can't see her eyes. Then she looks back up at me again, her face all serious; sort of hurt until I force a smile and she manages one too.

"Sorry," she says, and it's okay.

As it turns out, we're actually going to Gorleston rather than Yarmouth, which is where we get off the bus. The rich salt smell of the sea is in the air and we head straight to the beach, even though the sky has clouded over and it looks like rain might be on the way.

We sit on the sand for a while. It's quiet and there aren't many people around.

"I could live anywhere in the world," she tells me, "And as long as I'm near the sea, I'll be happy."

The next thing she does is get up and announce that she's going for a swim. Her dark swimsuit's hidden under her clothes, but she asks me not to look at her until she's covered by the water.

I laugh and say, "Mary, I've seen you naked for fuck's sake!"

"I've put on weight since then."

She waits until I give in and shut my eyes. She walks to the water and obviously I can't help sneaking a little look at her.

"You can look now," she shouts from the sea, and I open my eyes and watch her swim around for a while. She really does look happy and at peace in the water. It's like the weight of everything lifts from her. All the problems she's barely even told me about but I know are always there just disappear for that time. And the full wonderful truth of all she can be is shown to me again.

She shouts to tell me she's coming out and to close my eyes again. This time I do as she asks. Then we go for an ice cream and see what the time is and that we need to go home.

"I have to show you where I went to college," she says, suddenly.

I don't even have time to answer before she starts walking. All I can do is follow her as she takes me through the town, where I see an old man wearing a baseball cap with the words '*John Deere*' and a picture of a tractor on it. 'Only in Norfolk,' I think to myself.

Before we get to the college the rain finally begins to fall and we take cover under a large tree near a church. I take a photo of her on my phone. Her black hair's wet; a shining ocean of ink. Salt water and sand is on her skin and her face is even more naturally beautiful in the shadows.

The rain passes and we amble the rest of the way to the college. I've heard her stories about a lot of the friends she had there before. She always describes them as being "Properly beautiful," even though I can't imagine that she wasn't the most beautiful one of them all. I know that she just can't see that and maybe she never will.

We get the bus home and are much less talkative than on the journey there. We're also a lot more comfortable together too. Then I remember something I'd been meaning to ask her:

"Are you going to Joey's birthday thing tonight?"

"I don't know yet," she tells me, which usually means no.

"You should," I say, trying not to push things.

"I'll think about it."

She smiles, which is sweet but it's still a no.

The bus stops in Wortwell and I give her a hug and get out. It's good to finally feel like I'm close to her again. She's waving to me as the bus moves away, so I blow her a big overly-dramatic kiss. She laughs and then she's gone.

I walk back home slowly and check my phone for the first time all afternoon. Turns out that Emily's called me a couple of times, so I figure I really ought to give her a ring when I get back inside.

Then I see the text from Patrick:

'When you get back, come straight round to robbie's there's something you got to see buddy.'

I wonder what he's on about and I feel like I kind of have to see. I can't help myself. I turn away from home and head up the hill to Robbie's place.

CHAPTER 6

Waiting for the Evidentiary Hearing to start took almost as long as the entire initial Arraignment had taken to complete. That gave David some more time to consider what he would be presenting to the judge that day, along with the various possible outcomes of the sentencing. He knew it didn't look good. The crime was too serious for the judge to ignore. A prison sentence really was inevitable.

The question was whether the honourable Judge Vickers would be willing to take into account Charlie's guilty plea and the fact that it was a first offence. That was what David argued for and, to his surprise, his passionate defence won the argument. The six month custodial sentence was a great result and still a thoroughly hollow victory.

Before being taken away to begin his sentence, Charlie thanked David for his help and for believing in him. He was taken down by two large policemen and as he watched him go, David was possessed by the desperate hope that he wouldn't have to see Charlie like that again. The fear that remained was that it was probably already out of his control.

David always felt rather cut adrift at the end of a case and this time the feeling was further heightened by the sense that with no real victory, there could be no real celebration; nobody involved had got what they deserved. He considered going back to the legal chambers but given that it was half past four on a Friday afternoon, it hardly seemed worth the effort. It was time to call it a day, and a week.

There were no plans for the evening or for the rest of the weekend either, but he felt a desperate need to get away; out of the uncomfortably full, yet empty, streets of the city. He sighed to himself again as he walked. He missed his family, especially his kids.

There was no pretending that things with Jonathon weren't difficult; his son still hadn't found any reason to forgive him. Emily was wonderful though. She'd always been his little smiler and unlike her brother hadn't taken sides in the divorce. Of course, he would have understood if she'd sided with her mother. He'd been the one in the wrong after all; he was the idiot who'd ruined everything.

The doors of the Central Line train opened to him and as he stepped inside he could feel the true extent of his stupidity and all it had cost him. He wanted to escape. It was no good. He was trapped underground. Instead, he sat down in silence, calming his thoughts enough to dull the sharp pain of his guilt and noticing very little about the journey, the train or the passengers; not even the attractive red-headed woman sitting opposite him; only a few years earlier he would have realised she was probably far too young for him but still would have tried charming her into bed. Quite a few times it would have worked too.

Blindly he went on, boarding another train that took him straight back to Alveston. It was only when he was able to play *Born to Run* on the stereo of his BMW that he felt any better. It was a song that had a magical quality for him. It never failed to make him feel the way he did when he first heard it on the radio in 1975; the sense that as long as there was a road to travel and something still worth fighting for, there was nothing that could stop him. It was a feeling he loved and cherished, if only because it never seemed to last long enough anymore.

On the short drive home, he stopped off to get some fish and chips. Battered cod rather than rollmop herrings was definitely more of his mother's influence; his displeasure at how little change he got from a five pound note was more of his father's.

Back at the flat, David plated up his dinner and managed to eat all the fish and most of the chips. In a way, that annoyed him. He'd been relatively slim all his life, despite rarely eating healthily or looking after himself in any way. The last few years had suggested that he was going to pay for this though; not only was he unable to eat as much as he used to but he'd also started to develop a much more noticeable belly.

He leaned back into his sofa and drifted off to sleep. The sound of the telephone ringing woke him. He picked up the receiver.

"Hello," he said drowsily.

"Dad?" said the voice on the other end of the line.

David immediately felt more awake.

"Emily?"

"Why don't you ever turn on your mobile? I've left five or six voicemails for you since lunchtime."

"I. Uh…"

For several seconds David was confused; the sleepy fizz inside his head hardly helping him as he tried to work out what she meant. He'd had his phone with him and switched on all day. Then he understood. He'd had his work mobile, which he always left on in case someone needed to contact him about a case. Standing up, he went to the kitchen and found his other mobile phone sitting where he'd left it, on one of the work surfaces.

James Eddy

"Damn it. Sorry Em, I forgot to take it with me today," he explained.

She didn't say anything for a few moments. He could tell that she was annoyed.

"What's the matter sweetheart?" he asked.

She took a deep breath and when she spoke her words were slow and deliberate:

"I don't know quite how to tell you this but... Granddad's collapsed and it looks like it's pretty serious. He's in a coma."

There was numbness, a nothingness that rose up from David's chest and travelled through his bones to his brain. He sat down with cold sweat on his skin and no idea what to think, let alone say. Somewhere in his mind there was definitely some relief that his father was alive but he couldn't be entirely sure why that was. It didn't make a lot of difference to him.

"They resuscitated him at the home and got him to the hospital. He's stable now, so they told me I should go home for a while. They said they'd let me know if he got any worse."

Thoughts returned to David's mind. There was only one thing he could think to do.

"Right..." he said, taking a deep breath, "I'll just sort a few things out and I'll be with you in a couple of hours."

"No," she told him firmly, "It's late. Wait till the morning. At the minute I think they're assessing him and trying to work out why he collapsed. There's nothing you can do right now."

Emily was sensible and, in almost any situation, David trusted her judgement over his own. This was no exception.

"Okay. First thing tomorrow then," he said.

"Good," she almost sighed.

He could hear the strain in her voice. It worried him.

"Are you all right Emily," he asked.

"Yeah, it's just been a bit of a rough day... I'm really glad I got hold of you though dad."

"Well, thank you for not giving up. And try not to worry too much about your granddad. He's a tough old bugger, you know."

"I know."

"Right. You need to try to rest and relax for now and I'll send you a text when I'm about to set off tomorrow. I'm guessing he's at the 'Norfolk and Norwich' or whatever they're calling it now?"

"Yeah, near the Uni."

"Then I'll meet you there," he told her.

"Okay..." she said, "It'll be good to see you Dad."

"It'll be good to see you too Em."

"Night then... And see you tomorrow."

"See you tomorrow... Bye."

David pressed a button on the handset and heard the dial tone. He looked at the clock on the wall. It was just after half past nine. He made himself a cup of tea and turned the television on. He quickly scrolled through the menu onscreen to see if there was anything worth watching. Nothing much appealed so instead he took the time to throw a few clothes into a suitcase and went to bed.

CHAPTER 7

By the time I walk up the drive they're all completely wankered and the armchair's barely recognisable.

"Ta da!" Stephen says, and Patrick and Robbie start giggling like the idiots they obviously are.

As I get closer it gets more and more difficult to believe exactly what they've done since I last saw them.

The most obvious thing is that the armchair is now on a bread tray that Patrick has nicked from where he works. This gives it what he calls, "Three hundred and sixty five degree mobility". Robbie's ripped a whole load of stuff out of his car and they've stuck it onto the chair too; the NOS from the engine is attached to one of the arms and they've actually cut a hole in the other one to stick the car radio into it. On the bottom at the back of the chair is a blue *'Diverted Traffic'* road sign that they've managed to get hold of. The bloody thing even has a flagpole with a flag and a Barbie doll attached to the top of it.

Still, my personal favourite part of the entire design is the decision to 'decorate' the plain, pale fabric by sticking the heads of flowers onto it, which is meant to "Give it a more homely feel".

I shake my head and they're absolutely pissing themselves laughing.

"Can I just say that you've excelled yourselves." I tell them.

Patrick hands me a can of lager.

"I promise, it looks even better after a few of these," he says.

I look at Robbie.

"What are you gonna do about your car?"

He shrugs.

"It doesn't go anyway."

I shake my head, drink the beer and laugh some more at the absurdity of it all. Patrick's decided we should take the armchair to the party tonight. I don't argue. I have to get home to get changed and have a bite to eat. The three of them follow me back.

"EATING'S CHEATING," I hear them shout from the living room, while I'm putting on a new dark grey t-shirt.

I put on a denim jacket and check my hair in the mirror. Then I find a bottle of vodka to help me on my way and go to the kitchen to make a cheese and pickle sandwich. I eat and we all drink some more and pick up a few bottles of various kinds for the journey. Only the best generic brands of vodka, lemonade and lager for the four of us! We collect the armchair from Robbie's, along with some other supplies, and start walking along the High Road.

We've decided not to go the quickest way to Alburgh. The village is a couple of miles away and even more isolated than this place. We're already going to be late but if as few people as possible can see what we've done before we arrive then the funnier it should be. We go towards The Bell, past Dragon's house and walk round the corner along Tunbeck Road.

The bread tray was definitely a good idea but it is incredibly fucking noisy. Any sound is simply drowned out by the roar of the wheels and metal in motion and people are going to hear us coming from a mile off.

We cross the bypass without too much trouble and start moving downhill, passing a few houses and trees on either side of us. Then I see a large converted barn on our right but that isn't what the others have noticed. Standing in front of one of the red brick walls are four orange traffic cones. Stephen instantly decides that he needs to have one, so he grabs it, puts it on the seat of the chair and we all leg it before anyone else notices.

We slow down to walking pace as the road gets steeper and we have to try a little bit harder to push the chair. It's quite slow going but luckily it's a Norfolk hill instead of a real one. We take a breather and push the armchair out of the road and to the side, while we all have some more to drink. It's starting to get darker and I look out across the grey-green field next to the road.

Looking back, I see Robbie sit down on the chair with the traffic cone on his lap and then Patrick and Stephen try pushing him up the hill. They don't get far before Patrick sees something and stops.

"What's that thing?" he asks and I can honestly almost hear the grin spreading across his face.

It's actually a wooden post in the ground with a map of the local public footpaths in a glass frame at the top. It's quite a heavy duty thing and the wood is dark and thick.

We all look at him and he says, "Right. We've got an armchair, a radio, a NOS, a flag, a roadsign, a Barbie doll, and a traffic cone... But we haven't got a map. Do you think we might need this?"

I grin and turn away from him and start pushing the armchair again. I just about manage to say, "No, I think were fine," when I hear the sound of an almighty crack somewhere behind me. I turn and see Patrick and Stephen ripping the post out of the ground. It's a ridiculous sight and I double up into the back of the armchair because I'm laughing so hard. I turn back and see the look of triumph on Patrick's face as he carries the post over, dumps it on the chair, and keeps on walking.

I have another drink and leave it to Stephen and Robbie to keep pushing. At the top of the hill it levels out again and I know we haven't got much further to go. I check my phone for the time and see that Emily's called again and remember that I forgot to call her back earlier. I'll just have to do it tomorrow. Too late now, it's already half nine.

I call Cassidy to tell her we're about to arrive and that everyone should come out into the car park of the Village Hall.

"Time for you to make your big entrance Gombo," Patrick tells me.

He then gets me to sit on the armchair while Robbie and him push me the final hundred or so yards of our journey. As they do this, Stephen walks just ahead of us waving the wooden post above his head with one hand and using the traffic cone as a megaphone to proclaim loudly and ludicrously, "HEAR YE, HEAR YE. GOMBO IS HERE, YOUR KING IS ARRIVING".

We turn right into the car park and find out that pretty much everyone has come outside to see the arrival of four drunken morons.

"We've brought you a present," I say to Joey, "Happy Birthday mate!"

I can't say that he's all that pleased but, obviously, once he sees the sheer blinding attention to detail in the design he can't fail to be impressed.

At the same time, when Bear sees it he is pretty pissed off, which I'd guess was Patrick's aim all along.

"You stole my idea," Bear says to us.

This isn't strictly true of course.

"No," I tell him, "I think you'll find that your idea was to ride a sofa down a hill... This is quite clearly an armchair."

"Yeah," Patrick adds, "And this has got flowers, a '*Diverted Traffic*' sign, a NOS. And your idea had none of those things."

Bear lets it drop surprisingly quickly. Patrick always seems to find a way to get him to back down. Although, it's usually just by out stupiding him.

We leave the chair to anyone who fancies a ride on it and go to the bar.

I soon find my good friend Cassidy and give her a big cuddle. I've not seen her in a while, so we really start hitting the vodka properly tonight; just like old times. I'd almost forgotten how much of that stuff Ol' blondey blue eyes can put away and neither of us ventures far from the bar for about forty five minutes. We get through quite a few doubles in that time.

That's when Dragon arrives. The surprise isn't that he's late; it's more that he walks in carrying a goldfish in a clear bag. He doesn't say where he got it from and he doesn't have to explain why he's brought it. As usual, it's just another prop to help him pick up women. Tonight is almost perfect for him. There's just enough girls here that he hasn't slept with, who don't know about his reputation or his long term girlfriend, and who are also drunk enough to want to know about the fish; within minutes you can tell it's inevitable that he'll be showing one of them all his tattoos and piercings later.

I step away from the bar for a bit and get chatting to Sophie, and Rachel, which is cool because I've not seen either of them for a while and we've always got on really well. Sophie and Patrick have always had a bit of a thing between them and that is a bit awkward because she's Robbie's ex. Nothing's happened yet but every time they're together it feels like there's definitely the potential for disaster.

Personally, I've always preferred Rachel anyway. She's just so odd and fucked up that I guess I was always gonna like her. She makes me think of the time I was at high school and I'd stay up till about three in the morning watching these weird, clever French and Spanish movies. One of the best ones was a film called L'Appartement and she kind of reminds me of Romane Bohringer, who was one of the actresses in it. I think it's probably because she isn't the most beautiful girl in the world but she is sort of deliciously strange and outrageously sexy. We keep drinking and talking. She's wearing a short white dress with a little lace at the neck, and she's flirty and fun and getting drunker by the minute.

Then Patrick and Allen come up to me, chuckling about something.

"Someone's spiked Bear's beer," Allen tells me.

I look over to see the wreckage of my friend on the other side of the hall.

"Doesn't look like that'd be too hard," I reply.

Then they really start laughing. I'm confused. I look at Rachel and shrug.

"They've given him Viagra."

"Oh Jesus!"

I shake my head and almost suggest that someone should give him a hand. I manage to stop myself but I can't help laughing a little bit. I look at Patrick.

"Ya see, don't pretend you're above all this," he says, "You're just as bad as the rest of us..."

He grins and pretends to storm off, before shouting back at me, "GROW UP WILL YA!"

Me and Rachel go over to poor old Bear to check he's okay. There's a few crisp crumbs in his beard. Other than that he doesn't seem so bad, or at least he doesn't seem any worse than he normally is after a few hours of heavy drinking.

I still decide to check with Cassidy. She's like the designated grown up of our little group, even though she's quite a lot younger than most of us.

"I think he'll be fine," she says, "But given the state of him it's a bit of a waste of Viagra."

He's not the only one looking rough by then though. In fact, most of us are looking in a pretty bad way, so it's probably just as well that it's almost time to go. There's just enough time for Joey to bring the armchair onto the dancefloor and properly illustrate Patrick's claim about the three hundred and sixty five degree mobility, while 'YMCA' is playing. I'm pleased. It looks like Joe's had a good night.

Another drink and it's time to leave but when everyone eventually shuffles out of the hall, we don't really go anywhere for a while; all too drunk and lazy to even move, at least until some bright spark tells Allen to push Patrick along the road in the armchair with his new Mercedes. It's an idea that goes well for almost five seconds. That's when Patrick and the armchair veer off course and end up flipping over into a ditch.

Naturally enough, he's fine. It's the chair that takes most of the punishment in the crash; the *'Diverted Traffic'* sign is falling off the back and the flagpole has come loose. He manages to pull the chair out of the ditch and leaves it on the grass verge. Then he grabs the pole and the Barbie doll and walks back to the hall.

I try to check that he's all right but there's no need. He's so drunk he probably couldn't feel anything anyway.

"Baseball," he shouts and throws the Barbie to Robbie.

Patrick readies himself, winding up and using the pole as a baseball bat. The people behind him move out of the way and Robbie throws the doll at him. He swings the pole, and surprisingly, he connects perfectly with Barbie. She flies straight back towards Robbie's head and he ducks only just in time. The problem is that he's standing in front of the glass framed notice board that hangs on the wall of the village hall. Predictably, the force of the impact smashes the glass. Robbie picks up the doll and Patrick looks at me.

"Time to go," he says with a shrug and a grin.

The car park empties bloody quick after that. The designated drivers shift some home and others to the after party at Bulmer's. I see Bear starting to walk back, limping so obviously that it's almost like he's got a wooden leg – which I suppose he has in a manner of speaking.

I figure that going with him is probably the right thing to do. It's not a lot of fun walking that far on your own, especially if you're in such obvious discomfort. I'm still pretty glad when Rachel tells Sophie she's going to walk back with me.

We leave the others to it and start walking. Bear is a bit more coherent than earlier but he's still not making a whole heap of sense. And Rachel and me just carry on laughing and flirting and, almost without me noticing, she's holding my hand. It feels pretty nice but I don't push it.

Then Bear sees.

"Why don't you two just get on with it and get off with each other," he slurs.

I laugh at that and I think I hear Rachel giggling too. I must have imagined it though. She stops me, kisses me, and then pushes me into the nearest hedge.

"Fucking hell!" I hear Bear say from somewhere behind us.

He shambles on, leaving us to it.

I don't know how long we're kissing for, or how long my hands are in her black curls but we eventually decide to get moving again.

It's a pretty slow process because we keep stopping every few hundred yards to kiss some more. I've got to admit that it's pretty awesome.

When we finally get to Bulmer's, it's obvious that Bear has already told everyone what happened. A cheer goes up as soon as we walk into the kitchen. Poor Rachel looks embarrassed but doesn't let go of my hand.

I don't drink much more, mainly because it's really relaxed at Bulmer's that night. Cassidy's younger brother, Tom is there and he makes me fucking crease up. He's just so damn weird and tall, especially when he's drunk.

"Shall we make out," he says to me, and then leans in to within a couple of inches of my face before quickly backing away, "Nah, I couldn't."

He points to his pretty girlfriend Marie, who's sat next to him.

"You see this girl... I love her. I really completely love her."

"I know mate." I tell him.

It already seems like he's settled and I think that's a good thing for him. It's also pretty good for the rest of us. He's a good looking boy and he does tend to get the pick of the women whenever we go out anywhere. I remember there was this party at Allen's one night where Cassidy stole all of our mate, Dog's weed. I can't work out where the fuck Dog was most of the night, but five or six of us were sat in Allen's conservatory smoking for hours. There was literally nothing left after we'd finished with it. And the whole time we were there, Tom had this girl, whose name I don't actually remember, sitting on his lap. The thing was, he was barely interested in her to start with and it didn't get better as the night went on. Eventually, he had to tell her, "Look, this isn't going to happen. Go try it with Dog. He likes it." So she went off and fucked him instead; which worked out kind of perfectly for everyone because it wasn't hard to get him to agree that since Tom got him laid we should call it even for the weed.

Tom and me talk for a while until something pops into my head.

"Where's Patrick?" I ask him.

"No idea mate," he says, "Last time I saw him he was with Stephen. They were running up the road with the armchair... Then they stopped and just dumped it in a ditch and legged it in the opposite direction."

I figure they're probably fine. The night's winding down, so I take Rachel back to her house. I get a couple more kisses for my trouble and head back to my own bed. I don't want to push my luck with her tonight.

As it turns out I am so damn tired by the time I get in that I don't manage to get out of my clothes before I fall onto my duvet and sleep maybe as well as I have in years.

CHAPTER 8

When he woke up he was covered in blood. Witold was sitting on the snow beside him. They were alone and still in the forest.

"What happened?" Karski asked.

"I might ask you the same thing."

He sighed and shook his head.

"You killed them. You killed all the Sinistrians. I've never seen anything like it. You tore them to pieces and saved all those people."

"Where have they gone?"

"They ran off. There's bound to be more Sinistrian's heading here soon."

"But you stayed anyway."

"I need to get you to the meeting of the Home Army that I'm going to. We can't have someone like you falling into the wrong hands."

Karski didn't ask what Witold meant by that. The black blood and mangled remains of the creatures he'd killed told him all he needed to know. He was a weapon and that made him dangerous to everyone.

"We need to go now," Witold said to him, and helped him up onto his feet.

Karski's skin, clothes, and hair had been soaked in Sinistrian blood but, as he stood, he found that they had dried almost instantly. Witold started walking and he followed him. They didn't have to go much further before the trees began to thin out and a small town of red brick buildings appeared from out of the greenery. It was a town built in the shadow of a huge mountain and was entirely surrounded by a large fortified wall of stone and snow.

The two men walked along a dirt road with banks of snow on either side of it. On the right hand side, there were two signs. The first gave the name of the town: *'Warta'*, while the other had the words *'Beware of the Manterrosh'* crudely scribbled onto it. Karski looked at the second sign, confused.

"What does that mean?" he asked.

His question was ignored, as the other man kept his eyes on the sky, looking out for any signs of a Sinistrian attack. It was sensible but unnecessary and, once they were inside the town's walls, the streets and alleyways, and the oddly angled roofs of the buildings provided decent cover for the two of them.

Warta certainly couldn't have been described as bustling. The streets were deserted and most of the windows of the shops and houses were boarded up. The majority of the town's civilian population had already fled to the relative safety of the forests or had been rounded up by Sinistrian patrols. The whole town felt abandoned; even hope had long since departed.

Karski followed Witold until he stopped at the front door of one of the houses and knocked on it. There was a brief pause before it was partially opened to him. The man behind it recognised Witold and both he and Karski were swiftly ushered inside.

Beyond the hallway was a large room that Karski assumed would have once been the living room of the house. They walked into it and found that they weren't alone. The room was filled with nine or ten important looking men. They all knew Witold but Karski didn't recognise any of them.

Each of them eyed Karski with suspicion, with the only exception being a big, bearded, bear of a man who was standing next to the fireplace. He was older than Karski and Witold by several years and the grey in his beard was nearly as noticeable as the suit he was wearing; which didn't only look well lived in but the green, brown and red checked pattern somehow managed to be utterly hideous no matter what angle you looked at it from.

The man smiled and nodded to Karski before going to Witold and giving him a hug.

"It's good to see they haven't finished you off yet brother. It pleases my heart to see you alive." he said with a broad smile

"Thanks Salamander."

"How was it this time?" the big man asked.

"It was fine. I've had worse scrapes getting back but it never seems to be very easy anymore."

"Their powers are increasing?"

"I don't know. Probably."

He didn't say anything else and the concern on his face remained. Salamander looked away from him and towards Karski. For a moment it looked like he wanted to ask him something. Then he stopped himself and looked back at Witold again.

"And that's..." he began

"Yes it is," his friend confirmed bluntly.

Neither of them had the chance to say anything else. One of the other men in the room had begun to speak and the attention of everyone was immediately upon him. He was a tall, thin man with greying hair and when he heard his voice it was obvious to Karski that he was the most senior ranking officer in the room.

"Gentlemen," he began, "As you all know, we are here today to discuss what is happening in the world beyond our borders and what this could mean in our ongoing struggle. You all know Captain Witold and the job he does for us, so I will simply leave it to him to tell us what he has learned from the Alliance."

Witold nodded to the man. Although he didn't step forward, staying between Karski and Salamander instead.

"Looking around at you all, I can see the true gravity of our situation. You all feel like you're cut off and there's a good reason for that. Right now, we are alone. There is no help coming to us."

His words sent waves of shock through the room.

"But, what about the Alliance and the Curzonians?" the tall man asked.

"I'm sorry to say that we aren't the Alliance's priority, Colonel Miron."

"But what about the assurances that were given to Retinger?"

"They are principles for action and are not in any way binding resolutions. This is war. There are priorities and we simply aren't one of them. They will do what they can but they cannot commit to engaging in anything more major to help us."

"Not even General Wladoslaw?"

There was an unmistakable note of desperation in Miron's voice as he asked this. There was little relief to be found in Witold's response to it.

"General Wladoslaw remains completely committed to us and to returning to fight for our liberation. The problem is that he continues to be fully engaged elsewhere against the Sinistrian hordes. The Alliance seems to believe that if he is able to cause enough damage in those engagements then the Sinistrians will be sufficiently disabled to give us all the chance of victory".

Silence descended upon the room as everyone took in this unpleasant information. It didn't last for long before Colonel Miron spoke again:

"You did not mention the Curzonian's."

You're right Colonel," Witold told him, "And there is a reason for that which every Pilecki should already understand. It should come as no surprise to any of you to know that we cannot trust those creatures. They have spent most of their history trying to destroy us. Nothing has changed. They will only aid the Sinistrians in our extermination."

But what about the promises Necrosarea has made?"

"Necrosarea is a politician, Colonel."

"So is Retinger," Miron replied.

There was a murmur of agreement from most of the other men in the room; a sound apparently springing more from hope than any strongly held belief. Witold swiftly silenced it.

"But Retinger is also not a Curzonian," he told them simply, "Believe me when I tell you that I have tried to find evidence that Necrosarea's claims are not just empty words and that he truly wants to help liberate us from the oppression of the winged monstrosities. That perhaps he might even see us as brothers in arms in a shared struggle. Or that at the very least he doesn't intend to carve up Pileck for himself and oppress our people. I've tried to find proof of any and all of those things and I've found absolutely nothing to back up his words."

"I hope you are wrong Captain Witold." The Colonel said sadly, and Karski recognised that it was a hope that was echoed in the hearts of the other men in the room.

Once again, silence fell until Witold spoke again:

"I am sorry my friends. I wish with my whole heart that I could be standing here giving you some good news. But as I can't, all that is left to us is to strengthen our resolve, in the way we've always done when things have been at their worst. If we do that then we can still be the ones to turn this war in our favour."

"Well said, Captain." Salamander stated emphatically.

Colonel Miron acknowledged the big man's words with a nod of his head and then noticed Witold was looking towards him.

"I have another matter to discuss with you Colonel," The Captain said, with a barely noticeable glance at Karski, "Actually, there are several matters that need your attention and each of them is of the utmost importance."

Miron looked around the room at the other men within it.

"Please excuse us gentlemen," he said to them.

He walked out and Witold followed him without another word.

Once they were gone the other men in the room started talking amongst themselves. Salamander moved closer to Karski and playfully nudged him in the side.

It took him by surprise, although he said nothing and simply watched as the older man took a hipflask from the inside pocket of his hideous jacket. He drank from it and held it out to him.

"Drink?" he asked.

It was only then that Karski realised how thirsty he was feeling.

"Please," he replied

Salamander handed the shining pewter flask to him. He drank, savouring the taste of high quality vodka. He certainly couldn't fault Salamander's taste in drinks.

"I wish they would put on a buffet or something at these things. I'm starving" he said to Karski, "Actually, just some good quality bread would do."

Karski handed the hipflask back to Salamander and let him have another drink. After swallowing it down, the big man started chuckling to himself.

"But then I'm quite sure that you're already thinking I could probably do with missing a meal or two."

His laugh then proceeded to boom magnificently through the room and somehow the sound of it seemed to lighten the mood. Salamander possessed the kind of positivity that was wonderfully infectious.

In fact, the only one who was completely immune to it at that moment was Karski. He was feeling something else entirely. His mind had suddenly jumped into the future and he was seeing everything that was about to happen.

He saw Sinistrians descending upon the town and the house they were in. They were firing on all of them and burning the house down with flamethrowers. The scene went black and he was presented with the sight of himself strapped to a table, being cut to pieces; chunks of his flesh ripped from his body, with metal and muscle piled on in its place. He was an open wound with blood flowing from him as he was made into something else; into something truly terrible.

The visions stopped and he felt weak. He realised that he was leaning on the formidable bulk of Salamander

"Are you all right Karski?" the big man asked, as Colonel Miron and Witold walked back into the room.

He didn't answer. He couldn't answer.

"Witold! Karski isn't well!" Salamander said sharply.

Witold went to Karski and put his arm on his shoulder.

"What is it?"

Karski looked up at him.

"We need to go. There is an attack coming and no-one here is safe."

"Then we really ought to be leaving," Witold said.

All the men split up into groups to leave separately. Witold and Salamander went with Karski through the back door. They didn't run. They walked quickly into the road behind the house. Everything was still, but not for long. The sound of machine gun fire was close and all three of them sped up to get to a small covered alleyway on the other side of the road.

"They're coming for me," said Karski, his voice shaking a little as he spoke.

"Thank you, we are aware of that," Salamander told him.

"We need to get to the 'Deep Amnios'," Witold said, looking up at the Sinistrians flying overhead through a gap between the metal sheets that kept the three of them out of sight.

More gunfire followed; close enough to concentrate Salamander's mind.

"The shipyard!" he almost shouted, "Follow me."

Karski found then that Salamander was surprisingly nimble on his feet and could certainly move pretty quickly when his life was in imminent danger.

More Sinistrians seemed to be circling overhead but Salamander knew the way well enough to lead Karski and Witold across the town without breaking their cover; cutting through empty houses and side streets when they needed to and using the cover of the alleyways the rest of the time.

It was slow going but they eventually arrived at the place Salamander had described as 'The Shipyard'. It wasn't what Karski expected. There were no recognisable ships or boats. Instead there were long metal ships, similar in many ways to submarines.

"What are those things?" Karski asked.

"Terra Subs," Salamander said, "They'll take us underground and out of the Sinistrians' reach.

There were at least ten long, metal machines visible, with each of them seemingly rusting on the icy ground. To Karski's untrained eye they looked beyond repair and he couldn't stop himself announcing this thought to his companions.

"I've seen a hell of a lot worse," Salamander told him, calmly.

The gap between them and the nearest Terra-Sub was a flat stretch of earth about fifty metres in length. There was no cover overhead for the entire distance. They were going to have to run and hope the Sinistrians didn't get to them before they could get inside one of the subs.

They sprinted as fast as they could and had barely travelled ten metres before Karski was checking behind them. Sinistrians were flying in their direction at great speed. Salamander also looked but didn't stop running, even when Witold turned, raised his rifle, and opened fire. The bullet hit the nearest Sinistrian in its left wing, sending it crashing to the ground.

Salamander reached the Terra-Sub and, with a mighty effort, he unscrewed the top hatch and opened it.

''QUICK',' he shouted to Witold and Karski.

Karski was there within moments. Witold was still standing twenty metres away. He took a shot, which grazed the neck of another Sinistrian, before he finally turned and ran all the way to the sub. He climbed down into the belly of the machine and closed the hatch behind him. It was dark and the next thing they all heard was machine gun fire and the sound of bullets impacting on the outer shell of the ship.

''You timed that well,'' Salamander said to Witold, "And it's a good job I can drive this thing too.''

He pushed some buttons and the Terra-Sub came to life. The lights inside came on and Karski saw the grinning face of his older companion. He assumed it was an expression that came more from relief than anything else.

"Ah, here we go... We'll be safe once we're in the Deep Amnios".

There was the sound of more bullets on the outside of the sub. Salamander raised the periscope to have a last look outside. He smiled and turned back towards Karski.

"They're really quite keen to get hold of you, my friend."

"No kidding," Witold snapped, "Now, do you think you might be able to get us out of here?"

"Of course, you only had to ask."

He took hold of a dark metal wheel in front of him and pushed it forward.

The Terra-Sub lurched forward and down into the ground. Slowly at first and then more quickly, it smoothly submerged; beneath the ground and out of the reach of the Sinistrians.

PART 2

CHAPTER 9

At eight o'clock, David awoke to the sound of voices spilling from the clock radio beside his bed. He didn't move for some time while he listened to the news that morning. Despite being half asleep, he tried to engage with what he was hearing. It was difficult. It wasn't anything he wanted to hear; just confirmation of the beginning of talks between the Conservatives and Liberal Democrats that were described as "Very constructive".

"Sell outs," he said, out loud to himself.

He switched off the radio. Too distracted to really listen. He showered. It hardly helped, aside from the fact that he obviously didn't smell quite so bad. That morning had brought with it an overwhelming feeling of being cut adrift. Emotionally he was lost; unsure of exactly how he could and should feel.

In a way, he knew that was sensible. He was concerned by his father's condition, despite doing his best to detach himself from it. It wasn't something he liked to think about, and nor was the knowledge that even if his father came out of the coma he probably wouldn't even know who he was.

This was an assumption that came from bitter experience, and from the last time he'd seen him on the 22nd May 2008. Stanislaw Gombrowicz had been diagnosed with Alzheimer's in 1999 and his condition had deteriorated rapidly. David had thought he could cope with it. It turned out that he was wrong.

On that day in 2008, he had gone to the care home and spent nearly three hours with his father; playing cards and talking about nothing in particular. Then David had tried talking to him about his mum, Anne, and discovered the true extent of the old man's deterioration.

The tragedy that the truth revealed was that the love of his life, the woman he had been married to for over fifty years, and the mother of his only child was no longer anything more than a "lovely lady" whose name he didn't remember. That proved to be too much for David to take.

Of course, he understood that his father had no control over his mind or his memories; Stanislaw didn't think he was an old man in his late eighties, he believed he was actually an eight year old boy; effectively making him an innocent trapped in a strange world he didn't understand but which made only as much sense as it needed to.

That had done little to stop David viewing this inability to remember her as an unforgivable betrayal to the woman who had loved him. Nearly two years had passed since that day and he couldn't deny that if Emily hadn't called the evening before he wouldn't have contemplated visiting his father. That was another source of guilt, although, naturally, it didn't change anything. What mattered then was that, even if his father wasn't ever conscious enough to know it, he was going to see him again.

He dressed and ate slowly, put his suitcase into his car, and did a quick double-check to make sure he hadn't forgotten anything; then he locked the front door and texted Emily to let her know he was on his way. It was a little after ten and he thought that, if he was lucky with traffic, he could be in Norwich in about three hours.

He set off, following the signs towards Cambridge. Not rushing or taking his time, he found he couldn't stop his mind churning around all that the day might mean and have in store. He tried to concentrate on the road; to fight what his heart and mind were trying to reveal; the fact that what he felt about his father had become tied up with feelings of his own hopeless love and crippling guilt for everything that he had made his mother put up with; more than anything he wished she was the one who was still alive, if only so he could apologise to her.

The traffic slowed to a stop just outside Cambridge and all David could do then was sit and wait and miss her. He almost felt ashamed to admit that to himself; he was a fifty-eight year old man who missed his mum. But that was hardly the worst of it, because, by then, part of him actually blamed his own father for her death.

He was aware of how unfair that was. Although it was just another wrong he considered unequal to the unfairness of the last years of his mum's life. They were the years of theft. The years that her beloved husband, Stan, was stolen away from her.

He'd always been the strong one. Often largely silent, but undoubtedly strong, or even belligerent, and when he made up his mind there was no deviation from it. His illness had changed all that. And not just partially. The man he'd been before had effectively faded away; becoming not just silent but barely there at all. The man Anne had been in love with, from the first time she saw him dressed in his army uniform, was gone. All that was left behind was an empty shell that looked a lot like him and provided a constant reminder of everything she'd lost.

As far as David was concerned, that was what had worn her down in the end. She lacked the strength to survive without him and even came to resent everything he had become. David could see that it had torn her apart. He was hardly the perfect son while she was alive, but nothing he'd ever done, or ever could do, could hurt her as much as that. She deserved better. And at the very least, she deserved to be remembered.

To David, she had been a remarkable woman. Amazingly loyal and she had always defended him no matter what he did. His greatest shame came from knowing that this defence was often more than he deserved. It was simply unconditional and that was one of the reasons he'd never doubted that she loved him.

He'd often questioned whether his father actually did. Stanislaw Gombrowicz was an intensely private man. A man who kept his head down and gave little away. Even in the comfort of his own home, there were times when he was almost impossible to have a proper conversation with. If he didn't want to talk he stayed silent, while at other times discussions turned into the kind of lectures that David was never likely to appreciate. Perhaps unsurprisingly, that had often led to terrible arguments between the two of them.

Despite this, what David had really wanted was his father's approval. That was why he'd started studying the law. He thought it would reflect well on his father and make him proud; the positive reflection that came from a second generation immigrant making so good, so quickly. It never happened though. Any pride at his achievements came exclusively from his mum and, even after twenty five years, David still felt some bitterness about that.

As he sat in the car, that bitterness swelled within him again and this time it was immediately offset by a far stronger sense of regret. The time had come to make a choice. To keep carrying around the bitterness, the negativity and the poison of blame, or to let go of the past and make peace with the memory of the man who had been his father. David took a deep breath and understood that after so long, the weight of holding onto the negatives was too much for him. The conflict within him led him along the path of least resistance. Letting go had become his only real and sensible option.

Another deep breath and he started feeling better. It was only a first step although it was significant. The ugly haze of hurt feelings, held onto for too long, was clearing and some of the guilt was floating away with it, to prove that the tyrannical touch of the past may not have tattooed his brain forever. At last, David felt calm as he was able to simply sit in his car, wait for the traffic to clear, and accept some of the less bitter memories and knowledge he had of his father.

Chapter 10

'Strawberry Wine' wakes me up; giving me just a little waltz time strumming, coming from my Iphone, to ease me into the day. I feel pretty good considering everything. It's nine in the morning and I listen to all eight minutes of the song. I roll over and go back to sleep and the next thing I know, the phone's vibrating on the bedside table. It's mum calling. I pick up the phone and put it to my ear.

"Jonathon!" she says.

My mind's hazy but I can hear that she sounds a bit stressed.

"Yeah... Are you all right?" I ask.

"Fine, but your sister's been trying to get hold of you."

"Yeah, I know," I say, "I've been really busy."

"Well, she's on her way over to you now. Your granddad's in hospital. He's in a coma."

I sit up even though I don't really know what to say to that.

"Oh... Okay," is all I can manage.

The phone in my hand vibrates about eight times.

"She's going to pick you up and you can meet me at the hospital."

My brain clicks into gear at last.

"Right, when did she leave?"

"Only a couple of minutes ago."

"Okay, I'd better get ready… I'll see you soon mum."

I press the button on the screen to hang up the phone and head straight to the shower. Afterwards I get dressed and get myself some breakfast cereal. The house is quiet. There's almost always someone here but right now I'm glad I'm on my own. I eventually look at my phone again and see there are four texts from Emily from yesterday. "Fuck," I say out loud. The signal in this place is a joke.

I draw the curtains and let the light in as I sit in the living room and wait quietly for Emily to arrive. A few minutes later there's a knock on the door. I go over and open it.

"Hi Em," I say.

She gives me a hug then looks at me.

"Jon, why don't you ever answer your phone?"

"I'm really sorry. I honestly only just got your texts. You know the signal's horrible round here. And I was out last night."

"It's okay".

She's heard it all before from me.

"You ready to go?" she asks.

"Yep," I tell her, "Just need to get my shoes on."

So I do that and we head out to her car, which she's parked on the side of the road outside the house. She looks at the overgrown mess of the front garden as we walk.

"You know, you really ought to tidy this up a bit," she tells me.

"Yeah," I agree, almost without thinking.

We get in her little red Corsa and drive away. There's plenty to say although I don't feel like talking. Not that that's usually enough to stop me.

"I take it that mum's filled you in?"

"Erm… Well, she only really told me that granddad's in a coma."

"Okay… Well, he collapsed yesterday afternoon and it was really touch and go but the staff at the home managed to get him breathing again. Then they called me and when I got to the hospital the doctor told me he was unconscious. They let me go in and see him… He looked really, really frail Jon…"

I see tears in her eyes.

"It's okay," I tell her, "He's a tough old bastard."

"Yeah, I know… I just feel…"

"Guilty?"

"Yeah."

"Me too," I tell her, "I haven't been to see him in months."

She seems surprised.

"Really? I thought you were still researching that book about him."

"I hit another dead end and I've not worked my way round it yet."

This is the truth, just not all of it. It's really the same dead end I've had since the beginning. The same lack of evidence, understanding, knowledge, story. I don't know. Maybe it's just a lack of momentum.

"You could talk to dad about it?" she says.

"No. I don't think I'll be doing that," I tell her, more sharply than I really intend.

"He might be able to help."

'Fat chance of that' I think, but I avoid saying it. She always was a daddy's girl. I don't need his help with anything.

Her phone buzzes on the dashboard and she quickly grabs and looks at it.

"Dad's on his way now," she tells me, putting it back.

"Oh good."

"It is his dad that we're going to see."

She sounds annoyed. I don't say anything. He's definitely not worth arguing about. Then I get a text from Joey:

'Party at my house tonight. Turn up whenever.'

I automatically text him back:

"*No worries buddy, I'll be there.*'

There's only the sound of the engine as I put my phone away and Emily concentrates on the road. Then she glances over and I can see that any annoyance has passed.

She asks, "So how have you been? And apart from the dead ends how's the writing going? You know, I'm always telling people that my little brother's going to be a famous author one day". She seems to be genuinely proud of me. And obviously I'm shallow enough to like that. Even though I'm equally obviously a fraud.

"Good. It's really good," I say, "Going well. Unfortunately, I was planning to do some writing during the course of today... But some things are more important."

I'm lying to her in just about every possible way. I had thought about doing some writing but, other than the fact I've got a small advance for my book, it's not going well at all. Essentially, I've written fuck all. I've literally got no idea what the story really is or needs to be or even the best way of writing it. Or, at least, I haven't yet. I know I need to get a move on, I think my agent's getting tired of the excuses and delays. And I kind of owe her for sticking by me when no-one decided to publish my first book. She's put her neck on the line, and I've been out getting pissed.

Sometimes, it kind of makes me wonder why I wanted to be a writer in the first place. I've pretty much always had a decent vocabulary I think; ever since I started reading encyclopaedias for fun when I was about 11 or 12. And when I got a thesaurus I really was well away. That's what turned 'guilt' into 'contrition', 'regret', 'remorse', 'shame'; or, 'anger' into 'annoyance', 'irritation', 'dismay', 'disgust', 'exasperation' or whatever. Mum always says that I love words and making use of them. She probably just means that I talk too much.

Really, I'd have liked to have been a musician or something like that. I was always a sucker for stories in songs and that was really what I wanted to do most. The problem was that I couldn't learn to play anything to any decent level; not like Emily, she picked up the guitar really quick, it's just she's never been that interested in it as anything more than something to do for fun.

I think I'm interested in stories more than anything though. Even at school, my favourite teachers were the ones that used their words to paint pictures in my imagination, and my best friends were the ones who told jokes or span yarns. As I've got older, I've surrounded myself with people that are storytellers; most of my friends are much better at telling them than me as well.

Now, writing's just kind of become something that I do, or that I say I do anyway. I like telling people I'm a writer. It feels like something that's worthwhile and it sounds a lot better than simply being a mouthy drunk.

I look away and then back at my sister. Changing the subject seems like a good idea. I don't want to think about these things now.

"And how are you?" I ask, "Your new bloke better be treating you all right!"

This is as close to brotherly concern as I can manage. It's never really been my strong point.

"Oh Oliver's great. And I'm great and yes he's treating me very well thanks."

I don't ask anymore. There's nothing more I need to know.

She sticks a CD on. The newest Spiritualized record, which she knows I've already got, so she knows I like it. Actually, if it wasn't for Emily I might not have ever listened to them or a whole load of other bands and singers that I like. That's one of the benefits of having an older sister with really good taste. Actually, it's like with most of the women I've ever known. They've all tended to have much better taste in things than I do, so I've found it's easier to just copy them.

We pass Harford Bridge and 'Baby, I'm Just a Fool' starts playing.

"I loved this from the first instant I heard it," I tell her.

"I know, awesome isn't it," she agrees.

I know it's hardly in depth, but talking about music with Emily is one of the things I really miss now we aren't living in the same house. There are a lot of things that drive me mad about sharing a house with her but that was always something I enjoyed even though we tend to look at or listen to things differently.

What it comes down to is that I'm basically more obsessive than she is. I'll totally immerse myself in music by a particular band or musician and then look even further outside of that; so I wouldn't just listen to everything Spiritualized ever released but also to Spacemen 3 and to Sonic Boom's solo stuff. That way I get to see how it all links together. Although it is stupidly more expensive, I prefer it like that.

The two of us listen quietly until the controlled chaos of something close to a free jazz flourish takes the song to its end and we drive into the hospital car park. She turns the music off, parks the car and we get out. Following the signs, we soon find our way to Intensive Care. Mum's waiting for us and she gives us both a hug. She looks quite upset. She always liked my granddad.

"Are you two all right?" she asks.

We both tell her that we're fine and then, for no reason, we sort of stand around waiting to do what we've come to do.

"Should we go in then?" Emily eventually asks.

I suddenly realise that I'd rather not. I'm afraid and my throat's dry. I still nod and look to mum. She does the same. I follow behind the braver ones and we all walk into the room.

CHAPTER 11

Beneath the ground the Terra-Sub floated on, lights shining through the darkness. Inside, it was rather cramped although Karski, Witold, and Salamander were at least able to sit down.

When they had reached a safe distance away from the shipyard, Salamander had opened several porthole windows at the front of the sub, allowing them to see out into the Deep Amnios of the underground. And, at that moment, this was what Karski was staring at.

He found it completely fascinating. Geometric shapes in yellow, orange, purple, blue, green, and red floated through the darkness. They weren't faces in the dark. It was more that they were echoes of something primeval and forgotten that moved slowly around and between the roots of the world above.

Transfixed, Karski could hardly remove his gaze from the colours and shapes. And he barely even noticed when Salamander asked Witold, "Where exactly are we meant to be going?"

"We have to go to Vistula," the other man replied, "There are things I must explain to you my friend. There are things I must explain to both of you."

Karski didn't look away from the Deep Amnios but still nodded and said, "I came from Vistula. I had to leave my family there."

"I know," Witold told him.

Salamander cut the Terra-Sub's engines and didn't speak. He understood when Witold had something important to say and also that it was best to stay quiet when he did.

"There are a lot of things I already know about you Karski. Obviously, there are also a number of gaps in my knowledge, as I suspect there may also be in yours. What you ought to know is that the Sinistrians want you because they believe you to be the single most dangerous and powerful weapon of this war. They believe that you can become The Manterrosh, which is a creature, or machine, with the power to destroy everything it sees. If they can find a way to control it, to control you, they believe that they will be undefeatable."

Karski did his best to understand this information, as he watched a red neon cage floating through the dark outside.

"Why Vistula then?" Salamander asked.

Straight away, Karski knew that what Witold had said had come as no surprise to the older Pilecki. His voice was too relaxed for him to have been anything other than prepared for it.

"I informed Colonel Miron earlier that, while I was away, I received reports that the Sinistrians are transporting Pilecki civilians out of our cities and into camps, where they are then systematically processed and murdered... I refuse to stand by and simply let that happen. In conjunction with plans drawn up with the help of the Alliance, the Colonel has given me permission to bomb the train lines at the central hub of Vistula... That should be enough to disrupt what they are doing, although we can't possibly hope to stop them completely... However, what the Colonel doesn't yet know is that this is only the first part of my real mission..."

Karski had stopped looking outside. All his attention was on Witold as he carried on speaking:

"It has become obvious to me that as a people we can't stand alone in this war and hope to still be the same at the end as we were when it began. The Alliance must be forced into becoming more involved in our struggle. I believe that if they were given cast iron, first-hand proof of the atrocities being committed by the Sinistrians on our people then they would have to send us more help."

There was certainty in what he said and a steely determination that Karski couldn't help being impressed by. Passionate and still clear, fear could do nothing to cloud this man's beliefs.

"What are you going to do Witold?" Salamander asked, obviously concerned by what he was hearing; looking directly at his friend, he let him explain.

"In the middle of all the disruption we cause in bombing the train tracks, I will stow away on a train to get myself inside one of the camps. I have to see exactly what they are doing to our people. Then I'll have to escape and report back to the Alliance."

Witold stopped talking and Karski shook his head, shocked at the sheer audacity of what Witold was suggesting.

"I think you may be the bravest man I have ever met," he told him.

Salamander wasn't so easily impressed:

"Or perhaps the most stupid... What chance do you really think you have of pulling this off? Even if you were to get inside one of the camps, you'd never get out alive."

"I've got to try."

"But it's suicide."

"Doing nothing would be suicide, but it would be suicide for all of us. Without the help of the Alliance we're as good as doomed."

By then, the cramped interior of the Terra-Sub seemed to have become even smaller; shrinking down to little more than the three men inside it. There was silence as Salamander took in his friend's words.

"All right," he eventually said, "How exactly do you think you're going to be able to get yourself onto one of those trains?"

Witold turned to Karski and simply said, "Him".

"You want to use him? You want to use the man that might well be The Manterrosh, as some kind of distraction!"

"That's who they're looking for and that's why it'll work... Once I'm on the train they aren't likely to take much notice of an extra Pilecki heading off towards his doom."

"And what about Karski?"

"I think there's a good chance that he's already too powerful for them to control. I've seen him kill at least ten of those things in one go. He tore them apart with his bare hands, Salamander. And if he is that powerful then he could be the weapon that turns the war in our favour."

"And what if you're wrong."

"Then I know he's in safe hands with you protecting him," he replied.

Salamander shook his head and a smile reluctantly appeared on his face.

"I had a horrible feeling you might say that," he said, "So, what do you think about this plan then, Karski?"

There wasn't a doubt in his mind.

"I think that if Captain Witold is willing to make such a bold and brave sacrifice then I'm willing to do the same."

"Then I will not argue with the majority," said Salamander, "I just hope that any bravery or sacrifice isn't going to have to be made on an empty stomach."

Witold smiled. He was always able to rely on the great Salamander for his bravery, as well as his ability to think of food no matter what the situation happened to be. The big man switched the engines on and the sub began to glide forward again; around, between, and through the beautiful shapes and roots in the dark.

"We must contact the Home Army in Vistula so that we can gain some kind of safe passage through the city. We might even be able to find some decent food and drink there too," Witold declared, with a nod towards his friend.

"Best try the radio then," Salamander told him, pointing to some buttons next to where Karski was sitting.

Karski touched one of the buttons and a red glow emanated from it as words he didn't understand poured, from unseen speakers, into the Terra-Sub:

"Et omnium circumstantium, quorum tibi fides cognita est, et nota devotion: pro quibus tibi offerimus, vel qui tibi offerunt hoc sacrificium laudis, pro se, suisque omnibus, pro redemption animarum suarum, pro spe salutis et incolumitis suae; tibique reddunt vota sua aeterno Deo, vivo et vero."

There was something about the words that he recognised but he had no idea what it was. Evidently, Witold heard nothing of any significance.

"White noise," he said, and the words stopped immediately.

He moved over and pressed another button. For a few seconds there was nothing except static and silence. Then a voice crackled through the radio waves.

"That sounds like the frequency," Salamander declared.

"Hello, this is Captain Witold. I am looking for somewhere safe to land inside of Vistula. I have a precious cargo for our struggle. So, I seek your assistance."

There was quiet again for a moment before the voice returned. This time it was much clearer:

"Captain Witold, this is General Bialoszewski. I have been told of your mission by those close to Colonel Miron. My men and I will assist you in any way we can... There is an area near to the football stadium in the city that has been cleared of people meaning that those dreadful winged deformities no longer patrol it... It should be easy enough for you to find. We will track your movements and meet you there in due course."

The radio fell silent.

"Do you think you can find that football stadium?" Karski asked Salamander.

"That's what the radar is for," he told him, "Should even be able to see if any Sinistrians are on the ground nearby. And if there are we can hold tight until they aren't, if you take my meaning. We're safe enough from them down here. Sinistrians can't breathe in the Deep Amnios. Not even in a sub, thank God.

It was only as Salamander told him this that Karski realised he already knew it.

"If it turns out that the spot Bialoszewski has in mind is no good then we'll just have to find somewhere else. It's a big city. Those creatures can't be everywhere."

Soon enough, the radar showed what was above them on a crystal screen next to Salamander. Witold stood, studying it intently as a green three dimensional image of the grass and trees above them turned into roads and buildings; with Sinistrian soldiers on nearly every street corner.

At no point did Karski even look at the radar screen though. Instead, he was looking out into the beautiful safety of the Deep Amnios again; at its rainbow of spiralling shapes He felt afraid. In the beautiful colours, he saw no visions of the future or the past, but, as the Terra-Sub began to rise up from the depths, he could clearly see much to fear in what was still ahead of him.

CHAPTER 12

The little that David had learned about Stanislaw Gombrowicz's life was undoubtedly incredible. A couple of years after his father was diagnosed with Alzheimers, David had done some research into the events of his life before he had come to England. For most of his adult life, he'd wanted to sit and discuss it with him; to find out the full story of his dad's life. Stanislaw was always very reluctant to do this and David had taken this as another sign of the distance between them.

Sitting, waiting for the traffic to clear, he realised how unfair that might have been. For almost the first time his mind was clear enough to look for another explanation; something more generous, more pleasant and sensible; stemming from empathy rather than hurt feelings. It finally occurred to him that the memories Stanislaw would have needed to unearth were almost too horrific to imagine. After all, his early life had been similar to that of many other Poles born in the early years of the twentieth century; a terrible, unstoppable parade of sadness, loss, violence and death.

His father had been born during a period when the Polish nation wasn't officially recognised. This meant that he was born in a village near Katowice in what was technically Silesia on October 20th 1918; only a matter of weeks before a new Polish nation came into being.

Like many people in Poland at the time, the Gombrowicz's were not wealthy, and, as was typical in a largely Catholic country, they were a big family; with four brothers and two sisters, spread over ten years, and all living under the same roof.

Stanislaw had been the second oldest of the children and became known for being a hard worker like his father and older brother. By the age of twenty, he was working as a baker, which meant long working hours but also involved plenty of skill and dexterity. It was a job he seemed to have liked.

Then everything had changed for both Stanislaw and Poland in September 1939. Germany and the Soviet Union both invaded in order to carve up the entire nation between them; with the Nazi's taking control of the west of the country, including what had once been Silesia, and the Soviets taking control of the eastern territories.

The affects were terrible and far reaching. Stanislaw wasn't Jewish but Hitler's doctrine of racial purity meant that, as a Slav, he was considered part of a subspecies. Racially inferior to the purely Aryan Germans, the Slavs were seen as little more than livestock and, as a result, he was forced to work as a slave to a German family somewhere in western Poland.

At some point he had managed to escape, gone on the run, and joined up with the Polish Home Army. From that point though, David had found very little about what happened to him other than that he had obviously managed to get out of the country before it became a Soviet Satellite State after the war ended in 1945. That was the year he arrived in England and when he met and married Anne Beecham two years later, his path back to Poland seemed to close forever.

He never took British Citizenship. He always considered himself to be Polish; a foreigner no matter how many years passed. As pleased and grateful as he was that Britain had taken him in, he remained detached because it would never truly be his country.

Even so, not even the fall of the 'Iron Curtain' in Eastern Europe in the late 1980's and early 1990's had led him to return to Poland. He claimed that if he had gone to visit the family he'd left behind there, then as a Polish citizen living in Britain, he wouldn't have been allowed to come back. Given his knowledge of the law, David had done his best to reassure him. As usual though, Stanislaw had dug his heels in, refused to listen and, in the process, managed to offend his son; who had taken it as a lack of trust or belief in his professional opinion.

The other possible significance of this had never occurred to David. Rational thought tends to be the first thing to exit when feelings are being hurt. As the traffic finally got moving that morning and he drove beyond Cambridge, he thought he understood. His father had been afraid; afraid of what he didn't and couldn't know because he'd already been away for too long. Too much would have gone or been changed by the years. He was a brave, strong and proud man and perhaps it was safer to not ruin the few pleasant memories he possessed, with a reality that would never be able to match them.

Except that David realised then that it couldn't just have been about landmarks and memories; it had to be about people too and also about making a choice. It was a choice that was simple and also would have been very painful to make; the choice between his extended Polish-Catholic family of literally dozens, and his smaller English family of Anne, David, Emily and Jonathon. As much as he'd loved his country and the people he'd left behind, he couldn't help loving his own family more. And back then, he had apparently been willing to make himself distinctly unlovable to prove that precise point.

It suddenly made sense to him. It was conjecture but it made sense in a way that nothing else did and David couldn't stop tears from welling in his eyes. He quickly wiped them away with his sleeve as he drove.

"He was such a difficult sod," he said out loud.

As something close to a calm breeze blew through his brain, he found himself wondering if Stan's life before he reached Britain might also explain why he seemed happy to do the most boring, mundane work. That perhaps the very nature of it was a necessary reaction to all he'd been forced to experience in his youth.

He had been a man who worked hard but he was actually much more of a craftsman than he ever made obvious to anyone outside of his home. He could successfully turn his hand to almost anything, and yet, he spent most of his working life doing tedious jobs, like endlessly soldering electrical wires into plugs. There was a certain amount of skill in it although it was definitely beneath a man of his talents.

It was honest work, at least, and David had often wondered whether his father would have been happier if he'd worked in a job that involved being skilled with his hands, instead of practicing law. He stopped that thought and allowed calmness to take hold of him again. There was little to gain by travelling too far along that line of thinking. It was probably best just to remember that his dad was a very confusing man

David drove on towards Bury St Edmunds. The traffic had thinned and he was making decent time again. The sun came out and he started to enjoy the drive; the journey through the green, flatlands of Norfolk coincided perfectly with the lowering in the intensity of his feverish thoughts.

Diss was the next familiar name that he saw on a road sign. He didn't make any attempt to stop and see what the years had done to the place though. He was already taking a detour from the quickest route to Norwich and within twenty minutes he was driving through Harleston.

It had been at least three or four years since he'd last been there. It had definitely changed too. There were more houses on the way in and out of town; newly built and identikit, functional homes. There were more charity shops, more takeaways, and more places to get a haircut. Despite this, there were certain landmarks that remained pleasantly familiar - the Magpie Hotel on the marketplace, the clocktower, and Monty's chip shop all seemed to be stuck in a time warp. David only wished he was half as well preserved.

He didn't stop; passing Lush Bush on his left and an oversized chicken in a field just before the Redenhall roundabout. David smiled at the thought that 'The Chicken of the East' was Norfolk's answer to 'The Angel of the North'. He thought it could certainly count as 'Normal for Norfolk'.

Beyond the roundabout the road rose up a little and he slowed slightly to look at the imposing and impressive sight of Redenhall church on his right-hand side. He sped up again and barely a minute later he was in Wortwell; slowing to pass his parent's old house.

After his mum had died, Stanislaw had lived there on his own for nearly three years. Things had been fine until he almost managed to kill himself by leaving the oven on all night; when one of his carers checked on him the next morning they were hit by the overwhelming smell of gas and it became clear just how lucky it was that Stan had stopped smoking several years earlier. Even so, it still took most of that day to air out the house, and the smell of gas had stayed on his clothes for nearly a week.

After that, David had decided that it wasn't safe to let him stay there on his own. More permanent and constant help was needed and so he took steps to have his father placed into the safety of a care home in Harleston; that way he could still get out and about and see the people he knew, while always remaining supervised and looked after. At the same time, he also had the bungalow signed over into his own name and he'd then seen to it that Emily and Jonathon had moved in.

He thought it was the right thing to do, even though Emily hadn't been able to stay there for very long because she'd needed to move closer to where she was working in Norwich. As far as he knew though, Jonathon was still living there.

Ironically, by then, that fact was almost the only thing of any consequence he really knew about his son's life. In a lot of ways he was a mystery to David. Five years of blank space after leaving University with a 2:1; it looked to him like Jonathon was just marking time. Emily had said something about him getting a book deal with a publisher but that was really just another thing that his boy could avoid telling him about.

He very briefly considered getting out of the car to see if he was at home and to offer him a lift to the hospital. Something stopped him. A lack of bravery. He sped up and drove through the rest of the village instead, turning left and then right onto the A143, which had once been the train line that went all the way to Lowestoft and Yarmouth.

The journey to Norwich was simple enough from there. For those twenty miles, it was almost as if a long-dormant autopilot in his mind was suddenly fully engaged and leading him on towards the place that had once been the centre of his universe. The difficulty only came once he got just outside the city. He still found it confusing to think that the Hospital wasn't at the top of St Stephens Street anymore. 'It's probably been made into flats now,' he thought to himself.

Heading onto the A47, David followed the signs to the '*Norfolk and Norwich University Hospital*', taking a turn towards Colney and the University of East Anglia. He caught sight of the hospital on his right and, after waiting for a few moments at some traffic lights, he drove into the car park. When he eventually found a space, he parked the car and looked for the Intensive Care Unit.

Then he found that he couldn't go in. He couldn't bring himself to do it. Suddenly he was afraid and he didn't know exactly why. He stood outside the building and waited. He did his best to compose and prepare himself for what was inside. It didn't do much good because he had no idea what to expect or even how he might react once he was in there. All he was sure about was that he wanted to delay it for as long as possible.

He suddenly wished he hadn't quit smoking nearly thirty years earlier. If nothing else it would have been a good excuse to put off going inside for a little longer. He thought about texting Emily until he realised that her phone would be switched off in the hospital. In the end, there was no sigh, just a deep breath to signal that he couldn't delay any longer, and then David walked into the hospital to see his dad again.

CHAPTER 13

He's a lot smaller than I remember. He looks a lot older too. He always seemed like a little old man to me, even when I was really young. Now, it's different because he suddenly seems to have got absolutely ancient. I shouldn't be surprised; he's ninety one for fucks sake. But I still am and I can see then that this might be a battle he really can't win. I look at mum and I know she can see it too. There's the same look on her face as I know I have on mine.

"What do we do?" I ask.

"You can talk to him, or hold his hand, or you can just sit here for a while. Whatever you feel most comfortable with really," Emily explains to me.

She's so much better at this than I am. I stare at all the tubes and cables that seem to be burrowing into and out of his flesh and I feel bad because all I want to do is escape. I quickly check the time on my phone and then I take hold of his right hand. I squeeze hoping that it will make a difference but it doesn't seem like there's much life or even hope left. At least he's had a hell of a life, I suppose.

"We're here for you Stan, if you can hear me," mum says to him, "And David will be here soon too."

I let go of granddad's hand and reach for my phone again. Mum sees me:

"You shouldn't have that on in here."

"Sorry, I forgot, and I just got a message," I lie and stand up, "I'll be back in a minute."

I go outside and text Patrick, asking if he can pick me up from here as soon as possible. About thirty seconds later, he texts back:

'*ok. About 35 minutes*'.

That sounds fine to me.

I go back inside. Emily is sitting where I was before. It seems to be her turn to hold granddad's hand. I'm relieved and a bit jealous at the same time.

"Sorry about that." I say.

"Have you switched it off this time?" mum asks.

"Yes but it looks like something's come up and I'm going to have to go pretty soon. Work stuff, you know."

Emily looks up at me:

"I'm glad you came anyway and I'm sure granddad would appreciate that you were here too."

"How is the book going anyway," mum asks sweetly.

She catches me off guard.

"Er, yeah good. Yeah it's getting there."

I really wish I hadn't mouthed off about it to everyone now.

"I think it's wonderful that you're writing about your granddad's life... You're a good writer so it should be a terrific book... "

I don't know what to say to that. I should be pleased at the compliment and should thank her for it. I'm too aware that she's biased and of how far away I am from doing justice to the man lying on the bed in front of me.

I smile at mum but say nothing and look over at granddad and know he's nothing like me; or is it that I'm nothing like him, even though we have the same blood in our veins. I genuinely know better than anyone, including him, just what sacrifices he made for me to be here now. The trouble is that just because I know the story doesn't mean I can actually write it; at least not in any way that he deserves. Maybe I need to step away from it. Come back to it in a few years' time. Or maybe I should just give up. Stick to freelance proofreading and writing short stories for magazines; or maybe even just the music reviews I do in the local papers. It'd certainly be a hell of a lot less difficult. Or it would once I'd eventually managed to pay back the advance that's barely been keeping me drinking without my friends subsidising me.

I say goodbye to mum and Emily, hug them and then say goodbye to granddad, not expecting to see him alive again. So, I look at him for a moment or two longer than I would have done normally. He seems peaceful and I genuinely hope he is. It's the least he deserves. Then I walk out, leaving the room and the whole depressing bloody hospital. Patrick's waiting in his car outside. I get in.

"What's going on?" he asks.

"Nothing. It's just my granddad's dying," I say.

He says nothing else and we drive back to my place without another word.

CHAPTER 14

The Terra-Sub surfaced in the road outside the football stadium. Witold opened the heavy metal hatch and got out first. Karski and Salamander followed him and they were met on the ground by General Bialoszewski and six of his men. Bialoszewski was an impressively tall man with short brown hair and serious dark eyes. Neither he nor his men were dressed in any kind of uniform. This was in direct accordance with Home Army instructions on the matter, which stated that, *'resistance should not be openly displayed until the specifically designated time'*.

"Captain Witold, Major Salamander welcome back to Vistula," the general said, "We should not stand in the open for too long. We do not wish to draw attention to ourselves. We can walk and talk."

The city was still as they marched through the streets and between empty, bomb-damaged houses. When Bialoszewski spoke he made sure his words weren't much more than a whisper:

"Everything seems to be pointing towards something major happening here soon. There's been a major clampdown on the civilian population and the Sinistrians have been even more trigger-happy than usual."

"They've been shipping the people out on the trains," said Salamander.

There was a look of surprise on Bialoszewski's face that lasted for only a moment before his cool and calm exterior returned and he spoke again:

"I don't know what you know but at the moment we have no information about where those trains are going."

"I have information I can give to you on this matter once we're somewhere safe," Witold told him.

"It isn't much further if we can avoid the patrols. But they've cleared out most of this part of the city so we should be fairly safe."

As they walked, Karski noticed that more and more things about the streets they were on were familiar to him; stirring things in his memory; things that he hadn't thought about or been able to think about for a very long time.

Despite everything around him being a deep, misty blue in colour, his mind and memory was showing him something else. Showing him the streets in Technicolour, the way they were when he'd been an eight year old boy running around in short trousers. The bombed out shell of one building had once been the sweet shop he'd gone to with his brothers and sisters; and he'd once kicked a football at the wall of the house on the corner for so long that the man who lived there, Mr Mejdek, had come outside shouting and chased him all the way down the street.

Karski realised that he was home. The house Bialoszewski led them into was the house where he had lived when he was a boy. It was also the house his oldest brother had inherited when their parents had died. They went into what had once been the living room. There were another seven men in it, Home Army soldiers surrounded by radio equipment and a disturbingly limited supply of weaponry. But Karski barely saw any of them. He walked into the room and saw that his entire family were there instead. His father was smoking a pipe and reading a newspaper, his mother was sewing, while three of his brothers ran around playing games and his baby sister slept in her crib.

Each of them faded from his sight, replaced by the members of the Home Army talking to each other. Bialoszewski was introducing Witold and Salamander to the others. They seemed particularly impressed to be in the presence of Salamander.

And all of a sudden, Karski understood why that was. Salamander was a very important figure within the Pilecki resistance movement and that was why he had been at the meeting in Warta. He had been the first Pilecki courier in the war. The first to make contact with The Alliance and, as a result, he was effectively the reason why the war was still being fought by the Home Army. His trips were what established the hope they had that salvation was still possible.

Salamander was not a courier anymore though. He was compromised; a figure too distinctive and recognisable after so many years of war. The courier and spying work had been left to the likes of Witold. Despite this, he remained a leader of men and a figure of great admiration within the Home Army.

"It's an honour to meet you Major Salamander," one of the soldiers said to him.

Bialoszewski turned to Karski, as if to let him in on a secret, and said, "Major Salamander's exploits in this war have already become the stuff of legend."

"I hope that isn't true," said Salamander, seemingly in response to both of these statements.

Conversation shifted to Home Army business and to Witold's plans. Karski let them all talk, quietly backing out of the room and away.

He went up the stairs, into the bedroom and saw something else he recognised. White linen sheets were on the three beds in the room; with the indentations in each of the mattresses still visible and obviously untouched for quite some time. That was the moment he knew his brother, his sister in law and his niece were all dead. Karski felt the sadness of that fact in the fabric of the room and chose not to disturb the beds. He lay down in the centre of the room, on the hard wooden floor and slept without dreaming.

When he woke up, Salamander was with him.

"How are you doing, young man?" he asked him.

"I'm all right," Karski replied, "How are you?"

"Fine."

He didn't really seem fine but Karski didn't question him on it.

"How long did I sleep for?" he asked instead.

"Not long. I thought I'd better make sure you were safe."

"Sick of being called a legend too I think."

"Is it obvious?"

Karski nodded.

"A little bit."

Salamander shrugged his shoulders.

"I was just doing what I had to do. We all do that. There are braver people than me who've made bigger sacrifices than I have... They're just the ones who've carried on living. Bringing up their children in the middle of all this and keeping our way of life going. They're the real heroes in this war. I only hope it isn't all for nothing."

He shook his head and Karski watched him for a few moments. With his positivity and enthusiasm drained from him he looked older. Even so, he didn't doubt that there was still enough fight left within the old warrior for what was to come.

"How did the war start?" Karski asked him, sitting up.

Salamander's eyes lit up and he smiled again, a simple sight that was still reassuring.

"You must be the only person in this entire country who doesn't know... And here you are right in the middle of it all about to risk your life to help people you can't even remember..."

He shook his head but his smile remained.

"There was no betrayal, just power and expansion and two terrible creatures outmanoeuvring everybody else. Erom Babylon and Necrosarea signed a pact to join the Sinistrian and Curzonian peoples together. It was a treaty that The Alliance believed, or hoped, would mean peace when it actually meant war... They joined together to invade us simultaneously. The Sinistrians from the west and the Curzonians from the east. We fought and we died. There was no chance."

"But I thought the Curzonians were at war with the Sinistrians too?"

"They are... But that doesn't mean they always were. And The Alliance have been trying to gloss over the part that Necrosarea had in the invasion of our country ever since he switched sides. We won't forget though."

"What changed between the Sinistrians and Curzonians?"

"It was never a pact that was going to last. No one really knows who caused the end of it, but Necrosarea is keen to suggest that it was just a matter of him coming to his senses."

"And you don't believe that," said Karski.

Salamander shrugged his shoulders again.

"He's hardly known for his honesty."

There was the sound of footsteps on the stairs and they both looked towards the bedroom door. It opened and Witold walked in. He looked down at where Karski was still sitting.

"Is everything all right?" he asked.

"Better," Karski replied as he got to his feet, glancing at Salamander as he did so.

"Good... It's time to get moving. I've got a train to catch," Witold told him.

"So, you're going through with it then?"

"Of course... I haven't got anything else planned. And General Bialoszewski is going to assist us. Everything should work out well."

There was a steely determination in his voice that dispelled the doubts Karski had about the plan. He nodded and looked to Salamander, noticing that he still didn't look completely happy. In spite of this though, he could see that the trust the Major had in his friend's judgement was absolute.

The two men helped Karski onto his feet and they left the room and went down the stairs. Bialoszewski was still directing operations in the living room. This time though, only three of his men were still there and the radio had been taken away.

"I've sent three groups ahead to scout. It goes without saying that there will be a large number of the enemy in the air and on the ground but we should still be able to put ourselves into a position to create the necessary diversion to allow Captain Witold to board one of the trains."

Salamander looked at Karski:

"We're going to create two more diversionary explosions," he explained, "That should guarantee that he gets on board and that we can keep you from being captured. Well… That's the plan anyway."

Even though Karski didn't find this particularly reassuring, he did appreciate Salamander's honesty about the situation. Witold was much less impressed:

"Major Salamander underplays his own remarkable gifts for survival and the abilities of General Bialoszewski's men. The winged monstrosities will not get the better of us, today or any other day."

"Well, it definitely helps that I've had a decent feed now," Salamander explained to him

And for almost the first time that Karski could remember since they had reached Vistula, Witold smiled.

"It was more like three men's decent feeds, my good friend," he said as he put his arms into the shoulder straps of the bag he would be carrying on his back.

"It's hardly my fault that I've got a healthy appetite."

Karski was made very differently to Salamander. The few hunger pains he had been feeling when he was in the Terra-Sub had long since disappeared. In truth, he was numb to almost everything by then. All that mattered was that he was ready. He simply wanted their mission to be done.

It was soon time to leave and all seven men armed themselves with pistols or rifles and left the house. It was still not very bright outside but the haze was a paler blue than before; more like it had been in the forest, in the shadow of the mountains to the south. After only a few hundred yards, Bialoszewski and his men took a turn to the right away from Witold, Karski and Salamander.

"Good luck," the general said to them, and then he and his men were gone.

The streets were completely deserted as the three of them went back towards the football stadium and where they had left the Terra-Sub. They were happy to see that it was still there and, from a distance, it looked like it hadn't been discovered or touched. All three of them still continued to keep an eye out for any signs of danger; their hands already on the guns that were concealed within their clothes.

A short distance away from the sub, Salamander noticed movement on the top floor of one of the tall buildings opposite the stadium. He whispered to tell Witold and Karski, and as he did so a Sinistrian flew out and came swooping down towards them.

Witold's rifle was raised in an instant. His shot was unerringly accurate. The bullet smashed through the creature's head, the force of it snapping it back. The Sinistrian hit the ground with a sickening thump.

There was no time to be relieved. Suddenly, there were more of them, and they were everywhere, moving in towards the three men. The Terra-Sub had suddenly become their only escape route, so they ran to it, with high pitched wails of ferocious intent filling the gap.

As Witold and Salamander frantically pulled the hatch open, Karski turned and faced the Sinistrians. The screams he uttered then were the roar of his pistol as it threw bullets out into the sky, cutting down six of them at once.

Salamander grabbed him and almost threw him into the sub. The big man followed him and submerged the vehicle to make them completely safe.

"Well I think it's fair to say that they know you're here now," he said to Karski.

"I thought that was the plan."

Salamander thought about that for a moment.

"Yes. Good point. Well done."

"We should check how the others are getting on," Witold said, pressing the buttons on the radio.

There was crackle and fuzz, white noise and not much else. Then suddenly there was a woman's voice speaking words none of them could understand:

"We're here for you Stan, if you can hear us... And David will soon be here too."

The voice was gone as quickly as it had appeared. The next thing they heard was General Bialoszewski talking to them:

"Captain Witold... Are you there Captain Witold?"

"Yes, I'm here. We are all on board. What is the status of our plans?"

"Very good. Everything is in place and we are prepared. My men wait for your word to begin the countdown. Do you trust Major Salamander to find the correct point of attack?"

Salamander rolled his eyes. Witold saw and smiled.

"I would trust him with my life." he told Bialoszewski.

"Good. That's what I thought."

"General... I want to thank you."

"What for?"

"For all of your help."

"There is no need. I'm not doing this for you. I am doing it for my country and for my family."

"You will hear from us soon. Maintain this frequency."

The Terra-Sub floated beneath the city. It was quiet. Only the sound of the engines could be heard above the breathing of the three men. They all looked at the Radar screen displaying the world that was above them.

When Salamander saw the train tracks, he followed them all the way into the centre of the city. As the train lines started to converge they could be sure they were close to the station. The plan wasn't for them to surface inside the station though. That would have drawn too much attention and would have meant dozens of Sinistrians were on top of them within seconds.

The ideal place wasn't hard to find. The train tracks, the veins of the station, went off in all directions into and away from the city. The sub followed four that were side-by-side; leading in the same direction and curling around and away from a white stone building separated into three parts, which was the main station terminal. The tracks then spread out and away from each other and came to their end in the main train yard.

Witold's plan was based upon careful timing and so, as they surfaced next to one of the trains, he spoke into the radio:

"Gentlemen, please let the countdown begin."

They each took a machine gun out of the sub's weapons store and as the three of them climbed out, they heard Bialoszewski say simply, "Good luck my friends". Then they closed the hatch behind them and stepped down onto the ground. They were surrounded by trains that weren't being used and they had to put as many of them out of commission as they could.

"It's a shame we don't have enough charges to blow up all these trains," Karski said, thinking out loud.

"Agreed," said Witold, "But all we can do is try to make every single one of them count."

Witold took his bag off of his back. He removed several explosive charges, and handed them to Salamander and Karski. There wasn't much time, so they split up, attaching them to as many of the trains as they could before setting the timers.

They had almost used the last of the charges when they heard explosions in the distance. That was the sound of Bialoszewski's men blowing up several of the larger train lines on the northern edge of the city. It was an action designed to disrupt and divert the attention of the Sinistrians away from the main station terminal.

Witold set the last of his charges and looked for Salamander and Karski. They stood only a couple of yards apart and about fifty yards away from where he was. He saluted to both of them and they did the same thing in return. Then he started running, back towards the Terra-Sub. Salamander had explained the basics of the machine and so Witold was to pilot it the short distance into the station; hoping that when the charges blew up in the train yard, more Sinistrians would be sent to investigate and that he would be able to surface in the station without being noticed. From there, he would be able to blend in with the other Pilecki already herded into the terminal for their transportation to the camps in the south of the country.

The main weaknesses of the plan were understandable. Witold had been aware of them but still considered it better to act then rather than wait for a better moment that might never arrive. It was a plan that was conceived out of desperation and over a very short period of time, meaning that the various possibilities for how events could transpire simply couldn't be fully considered. The biggest problem was that because the city was so completely under the control of the Sinistrians, they could not be entirely sure where the enemy would come from in response to Bialoszewski's bombings to the north.

As it turned out, they weren't particularly lucky. Enormous numbers of Sinistrians were ordered into the sky. If there was going to be any kind of resistance, they would try to crush it as quickly as possible through weight of numbers and their superior firepower.

They set out from every part of the city and when Karski heard the flapping of wings, he knew they were in trouble. Four Sinistrians flew over the train yard and the three Pilecki didn't have time to find cover. When they were spotted, the Sinistrians did what came most naturally to them and flew down to attack.

Witold didn't stop running. He had to get to the Terra-Sub. It was the best chance for all of them. At the same time, Karski and Salamander ran for cover by ducking beneath the trains to keep out of sight. It was a risky strategy and they were aware that what was protecting them might kill them at any moment. They readied themselves. Their machine guns were already in their hands and at that moment they were prepared to stare death in the face.

Witold reached the sub but couldn't open the hatch before a bullet passed his ear. He took cover behind the metal machine. All four Sinistrians had landed and had already turned their attention away from Karski and Salamander and towards him. They closed in and he was ready to make a final stand against them. He was about to jump up and open fire. He was too late.

Bullet's sprayed into the air from the machine guns of the other two Pilecki. The damage to their enemies was minimal but it was enough of a surprise to force them back into the sky. Karski and Salamander continued to fire and forced the Sinistrians away for a few moments. That was all the time they needed to reach Witold and take cover with him behind the Terra-Sub.

"Was this part of your plan?" Salamander asked him.

"Not exactly."

"What do we do now then?" he asked.

"We wait for a diversion," said Karski.

The other two stared at him as the first of the trains exploded. It was close to them and they knew that this was their chance. They jumped out from behind the sub and Karski and Witold tried to shoot down the Sinistrians, while Salamander opened the hatch. As more of the trains blew up, Salamander pulled it open. He glanced back and saw that another Sinistrian had landed behind them. Witold had his back to the creature as it took aim at him with its rifle. In an instant, Salamander pushed his friend out of the path of the bullet, and it smashed into his own chest instead.

Karski turned and hit the Sinistrian between the eyes with his next shot but it was already too late for Salamander. Witold stood in shock for several moments as more trains exploded around him; lighting up the face of the friend who had given his life for him.

Karski grabbed hold of Witold by the lapels of his shirt.

"GET IN," he shouted over another explosion.

Witold did as he was told and climbed into the sub. Karski went to close the hatch.

"WHAT ABOUT YOU?" Witold shouted up at him.

"I'M STICKING TO THE PLAN. NOW, DO WHAT YOU HAVE TO DO."

Witold nodded and let the hatch fall.

Karski stood back and watched the Terra-Sub fall back into the ground, and into the Deep Amnios. He turned around as the last of the explosions resounded through the train yard. He was completely surrounded by at least fifty Sinistrians, drawn to him by the flames and smoke.

Staring down at poor, brave Salamander, he was able to steady himself. At least fifty guns were trained upon him and he was prepared for the end. He only hoped it would be quick.

That was when he realised that he couldn't move and that the Sinistrians had outmanoeuvred him. From the ground a noxious black liquid was rising up and covering his shoes, legs, and torso. It was cold and had the putrid stench of death. It continued to rise up, over his body, covering his arms and neck. Then it was on his face and in his ears, eyes, and throat. Karski couldn't breathe, he couldn't see, and he couldn't hear anything at all.

CHAPTER 15

David sat in silence beside his father. There were green curtains that went all the way around the bed, cutting him off from the rest of the ward; and from more old men who were either slipping away or in-and-out of consciousness.

Two women were sitting opposite David on the other side of the bed. They were both quite lovely, even though they were over twenty years apart in age; both had long dark, wavy hair; blue-green eyes and pale skin. Not for the first time, and, on a lot more levels than he would have liked, David found himself glad that Emily took after her mother rather than him.

But looking at the two of them was just a way of distracting himself from the fact that since he'd arrived he had no idea what to do with himself; sitting there didn't seem to be enough. Being his father's next of kin should have made it easier to revert to viewing everything from a legal standpoint. That felt wrong though. It was too detached and wasn't how he was feeling that day. At the same time though, keeping emotions near the surface didn't come naturally to him; he wondered if it might have been different if his dad had been conscious.

His thoughts turned to the woman sitting beside his daughter. Melissa was a distraction he hadn't expected. The day had already been filled up with enough of his guilt without being forced to face more of his rather too obvious failings. To be fair, the two of them were actually on surprisingly good terms and she was always very good to him despite everything; but that didn't really help. The problem was that he felt he didn't deserve her kindness.

He was probably right too. From the start, he'd known that something wasn't quite right between them as a couple. She was a radiant beauty when they met but that had been the only real attraction for him. He'd had no interest in what she was actually like as a person. She had been the fantasy of what he thought he deserved; a beautiful woman that he could project his thoughts and feelings onto.

That was the sadness of it all. To him, she had never been a truly real and rounded person. Superficially, and, for quite a long time, that hadn't mattered all that much. He'd maintained the fantasy even after they were married. It only changed when Emily and Jonathon were born and Melissa had become something new. Rather than just a beautifully empty fantasy woman, she was also a mother and that basically meant that he could never again be the complete centre of her universe.

He couldn't deny what an ungrateful pig he'd been. David almost felt sick, knowing that he'd always been cursed with an ability to overthink things. And by doing that he had managed to convince himself that the wonder of Mel as a mother showed that she wasn't the same woman he'd married.

It was a distortion that went even further by making him question whether he was still the same man he had been when he was twenty five. There was no answer he'd wanted to hear or understand. David tried to tell himself it was only a midlife crisis. He soon understood that he was lying to himself and in the end he couldn't deny that it went back much further; and all he really wanted was the shallow thrill, the shallow need; to bring back the fantasy image of the beautiful young woman on his arm.

It took years but eventually the inevitable cliché played itself out. He left his wife and children for a younger woman. It was a relationship that lasted barely six months. And she left him because it turned out that he really wasn't the same man he'd been when he was twenty five. It was only then that he learned the true limitations of fantasy; their inability to get you anything you truly want and need on their own. That was how and why David had thrown away everything he should have ever wanted. And that had left him alone. He couldn't find any way to convince himself that it wasn't exactly what he deserved.

Putting these thoughts and feelings aside, he was rather touched to see Melissa that afternoon. It said everything about her kindness and compassion that even after everything that had happened, she still cared enough about Stan to come into the hospital and sit with him. David appreciated that. Although that didn't mean that he knew exactly what he should say to her; he was far too conscious that he didn't deserve her time, let alone her pity.

In the end, she was the one who spoke first.

"I'm sorry that you just missed Jonathon," she eventually said to him.

"That's fine, I'm used to him avoiding me," he responded, with a shrug.

"Oh no, it's not like that I'm sure. He's been very busy. Writing his book and things like that."

David actually liked that she defended Jonathon. It was obviously meaningless because they were all aware of the truth; so it was nothing more than a mother's prerogative to try to bend the truth to cast her child in a better light. It reminded him of his own mother.

"How was your journey dad?" Emily asked, trying to change the subject.

He was happy to oblige:

"Not bad… A bit of traffic near Cambridge but nothing too serious."

The room went quiet again, and the only sound was the constant, reassuring beep of the heart monitors on the ward. Looking at where his father lay, David felt himself start to tear up a little, his emotions rising to the surface, seemingly from nowhere.

"He looks so small and weak…" he said, "I never expected him to look like this."

Emily stood up.

"I know dad," she said to him, "None of us really expected it. But he is very old now."

She walked round the bed and put her arm around his shoulders. He looked up at her. Tears were in his eyes. He sniffed and wiped them away. Taking a single deep breath, he sat up and looked away from Emily.

"Have they found out any more about what's wrong with him?" he asked, as calmly as he could.

Melissa looked at him and caught his gaze with her own as she said, "The doctor's going to come and explain things to us as soon as he's free".

David gazed at her and then back at Emily, who was sitting on the chair next to his. He spoke again:

"I want you to know how much I appreciate you being here. Both of you have taken on too much of the burden of all this. I really don't know if I could cope without the two of you being here."

"It's okay dad," Emily told him immediately.

Melissa said nothing.

David looked at his daughter again and this time he smiled. Then a nurse opened the curtains and came in to check on Stanislaw; the frail, unconscious elephant in the room. She checked on the heart monitor and ventilator, which continued to make their encouragingly consistent noises. David did his best not to disturb her while she worked.

"Is the doctor on his way?" he asked, when she was finished.

"Yes, Doctor Sterling will be with you shortly."

She smiled kindly at him and left, closing the curtains behind her as she went. He didn't manage to smile back. It had suddenly struck him again that there could be no happy ending in this situation. That even if Stan came out of the coma, his mind was still lost. He would still be a shell of a man with the mind of a boy. David thought he understood how his mum must have felt in the final weeks and months of her life. And he couldn't help feeling doubly sad.

He tried to summon up all his strength. Telling himself that they could still make the best of it. He could still be a better son, if he got the chance to be. For a brief moment, he thought about praying before pushing the idea away; unable to see what good it would do other than to compound a lifetime of hypocrisy. It was something he hadn't done since he was eight, about something stupid and pointless that he could barely remember.

Before he was able to do or say anything else, Doctor Sterling had stepped through the curtains and closed them behind him. He was in his early thirties, tall and self-assured, with jet black hair, and pale skin that made it look blacker still. He introduced himself and there was seriousness in his voice but also a sense of calm that was exactly what David needed.

"What's the matter with him doctor," Emily asked, quickly.

"Well," the doctor replied, in a gentle Scottish accent, "The collapse and coma are almost certainly because of a viral infection, which is what we've been trying to treat. It's also possible that he may have sustained a head injury when he fell, which may be further complicating matters."

"So, what's the prognosis?" David asked.

"That's rather difficult to say at this stage. As I said, we've been attempting to treat the viral infection but so far he hasn't been responding to the treatment as strongly as I would have hoped. There could be a number of reasons for that and it may just be that he is, after all, a very old man. I wish I could give you better or more detailed information but rest assured we are doing everything that we can to get him better as quickly as possible."

He was just turning to leave when Melissa asked, "Is there anything more we can do?"

For the first time, his face relaxed into a smile and he shared it with all three of them.

"You can rest and look after yourselves for now. He's quite comfortable and I don't envisage any changes to that in the next few hours. If there are any we will contact you straight away."

"Thank you Doctor," Emily told him.

David listened, staring out into space. He blinked back into the moment and looked up at the doctor: "Yes, thank you".

Doctor Sterling breezed through the curtains, out onto the ward and was gone.

For a few moments, there was quiet. The sound of the mechanical rhythms emanating from the machines attached to the old man's body becoming clearer again; a clinical cold sound that suggested the ticking of time was the very thing that was keeping him alive. David didn't want to hear it.

"I'm not sure what to do with myself now," he declared.

"Well, personally I think we could all do with spending a little time staring at something other than these four walls and poor old Stan," Melissa said, "We can come back here tomorrow and see how he's doing. Hopefully they'll have something more positive to tell us by then."

There was no need for any discussion. Emily was already nodding her head and David wasn't in the mood to argue. He stood by the bed, took hold of his father's hand and kissed it. Part of him was romantic enough to hope for the fairy-tale and that something so simple might bring him back; like Sleeping Beauty awoken by a loving kiss. No such luck and no surprise. He silently cursed the cheap sentimentality that afflicted him and laid Stan's hand back down onto the bed.

He looked at him for several more seconds and then opened all the curtains, exposing his father's bed to the rest of the ward. Strangely, he felt a little bit better. Not being so enclosed had lifted some of the weight he felt he was carrying. He was still aware that it probably wouldn't last long.

He walked out of the ward followed by Emily and Melissa and didn't stop until they reached the doors leading out of the Intensive Care Unit.

"Do either of you need a lift home?" he asked

"No thanks. We both drove here." Melissa replied.

"I forgot to ask where you're staying, dad."

"I'm not sure yet... I'll find a Travel Inn or something."

"I'd let you stay at mine but there's barely enough room to swing a cat in there," Emily explained before looking at Melissa, "Mum?"

"You could sleep on the sofa at the house, I suppose."

"No, no, it's fine honestly," he told them, forcing a smile onto his face, "You've both done enough for me already, thanks... So where did you both park anyway?"

They pointed to the right.

"Well I'm just over here," he said pointing left, "So I guess I'll be seeing both of you tomorrow morning?"

"God willing," said Melissa.

"Indeed."

"I'll be here by half ten I think," Emily told him.

"Then I'll see you at half ten."

David gave her a hug and held out his arms to Melissa. She put her arms around him, offering comfort for only a few seconds before slowly backing away.

"Bye," he said, almost under his breath.

She looked at him, quickly waved and walked away. He did the same and very calmly returned to where he'd left the car. He got in and sat with his hands on the wheel for several minutes. Appreciating the quiet as he looked back at the hospital building his dad was in, and then at his daughter and ex-wife, still walking to their cars.

Feelings of guilt weren't far from the surface again as he looked away to programme the nearest Travel Inn hotel into his Satnav. It wasn't all that far. Just off St Stephen's Street, next to the newish bus station that he hadn't actually seen before.

He changed the CD in his car stereo. Swapping one Springsteen record for another; from *Born to Run* to *Darkness on the Edge of Town*. Then David drove away slowly, as the opening chords of 'Badlands' offered a vibrant sense of hope in a world that was falling apart. It was a sentiment and a feeling that he'd never understood or identified with more fully than at that very moment.

CHAPTER 16

I start drinking early. Patrick helps me. I'm on vodka and he's on beer. We sit around talking bollocks because otherwise I might have to think about other things. Stephen turns up but he's not drinking today. He's still feeling last night. I tell them what Tom told me. About them dumping the armchair in a ditch and then legging it.

"I had to get the bread tray off it," Patrick explains, "And we weren't exactly gonna take the bloody thing home. If Joey can't be arsed to keep the thing why should we bother?"

"How come you never came back to Bulmer's last night?"

"I got a text from Rosie and she's just split up with her bloke, so we went round to try and cheer her up."

"Fucking hell! What time did you get there?"

"Pretty late," Stephen says, "About two."

I look at Patrick.

"You must've been driving completely trashed."

"Nah... I was quite sober by the time we got there."

"Jesus, man."

He's a fucking idiot sometimes. So fucking reckless.

"It's all right. Don't worry... We managed to cheer her up," he tells me with a stupid grin.

We drink some more and I know I really should be doing some work. That was the excuse I gave myself for leaving the hospital earlier. It was okay to go as long as I did some writing when I got back. And I actually did have what might be a decent idea on the way home.

I still don't bother to do anything. I keep drinking and soon enough I'm too pissed to care. I switch to wine and Stephen goes home. He's not coming to the party. We don't ask and he doesn't tell us why.

"How are we getting there tonight anyway?" I ask Patrick.

He shrugs and grins again.

"I could drive… Unless you'd rather walk."

I surprise him and choose to walk. We're drunk enough already, so it gives us a chance to sober up a bit before we get some more drink and head to the party. It's only about three miles to Harleston anyway.

Surprisingly, I get a text from Mary as we walk:

'Where are you? I heard you were coming tonight.x'

'I am. I didn't know you were though. X'

'I thought I should since I couldn't make it last night. I'd quite like to see you. How long are you going to be? I haven't got all night!xx'

'Not long. Do you want me to get you anything to drink? XX'

'Surprise me. See you soon.xx'

We arrive in town about fifteen minutes later and head to Budgens. It's about eight and we know Joe's meant to be doing a barbecue. So, Patrick picks out some of those weird sort-of plastic, processed cheese slices to help out. And nothing else. Then we check out the drinks.

"What should we go with tonight?" he asks me.

"Don't know mate. I've got to pick something up for Mary too."

"Oh right. Not beer then!"

"I've already been drinking vodka."

"Good point... Will she drink wine?"

"Yeah I think so... And I'll just stick to vodka," I say.

"You're awesome," he tells me, "I'll just get beer for myself then."

We go over to the rows of bottles, lovingly laid out and glittering in the permanent light of the shop. I pick up two bottles of Asti, a bottle of vodka, and two bottles of generic brand cola. It doesn't matter, I'm hardly a connoisseur. He gets a twelve pack of lager. We both pay and leave.

We're about half way between there and Joey's when Mary texts again:

'Where are you?xxx'

I don't text back. We're almost there and a few minutes later, I'm pushing open the glass front door to the house and walking inside. We walk through the hall into the kitchen and find that Joe's managed to get a pretty decent crowd in. Bear's showing off his crazy good electrical expertise by setting up some sort of makeshift karaoke machine in the conservatory for later. And there's about twenty people outside, sitting or standing near the barbecue. Mary skips over to me and flings her arms round my neck. She's already pretty drunk.

"What did you bring me," she enquires.

I pull out one of the bottles of Asti from a lime green carrier bag.

"Some Asti. And I got another bottle for everyone else."

I look over towards the little pond and see that Cassidy's sitting on a camping chair, drinking; looks like another vodka night for her. She sees me and smiles but doesn't get up. I put my arm around Mary's waist and turn back towards the conservatory. I usher her through the door and follow her inside.

The Asti goes in the fridge and I take the vodka and cola out of the carrier bag. Mary opens one of the cupboards by my head, grabs a couple of glasses and puts them down on the work surface.

"And who said this was for you?" I ask her.

She smiles at me. It's such a lovely smile.

"Oh all right then."

I pour two large measures of vodka out and she adds a dash of the old generic to them. I drink and it's pretty damn good. Exactly what I need after the walk.

We go back outside and I see Patrick is sitting next to Cassidy, between her and her friend, whose name I can't quite remember tonight. What I do manage to remember is that she once told me that rich tea biscuits taste like headaches. I still can't quite figure that one out

Cassidy gets up and comes over to me to give me a kiss on the cheek and a hug. She's such a touchy feely girl and she's like this with everyone. In a lot of ways it's a brilliant thing. She loves her friends so much she could almost squeeze them all to death. The downside of it is that she's ends up being much too grateful to any guy who fucks her. She's such a lovely, pretty thing and it's almost as if she thinks they don't get anything out of it.

We all sit down together on the grass and Joey and Bear appear from somewhere with a load more booze and meat. We eat and drink and, about half an hour later, a load more people turn up. That's when Bear gets the karaoke going. Joey's the first up, singing 'Video Killed the Radio Star' as badly as it is possible to imagine. But it's his party so who fucking cares!

Mary's knocking back the vodka pretty rapidly and I try to get her to slow down a bit. She's not keen on the idea and I try to distract her by making her come indoors to choose a song for us to sing. That works pretty well until we can't decide on any song and end up going outside again. We sit on the camping chairs side-by-side just talking. It suddenly seems very dark in the garden and I realise that we're the only ones out here.

"Where's my drink? she asks.

"You finished it."

"Then fetch me another one, my darling boy," she says, mock dramatically and rather drunkenly.

It makes me smile but I shake my head.

"Mary you're trashed."

"That's probably true... And is that a problem?"

"Just go easy."

"You're a fine one to talk Mr Gombrowicz."

"That's probably true too... But I worry about you."

She sighs.

"I know ... And secretly I like that you do."

She moves to kiss me. I move away.

"This is a horrible idea." I tell her.

"Why?"

"Do I really need to answer that?"

"I don't know. I am quite drunk." she says.

"Let's go inside with everyone else," I suggest, unable to believe that I'm being the sensible one.

"But I like being out here with you."

I down what's left of my vodka.

"I need another drink," I tell her.

"And are you going to get me another one too?"

"If I have to."

"You do."

I get up and walk to the conservatory. I look back at her and say, "Thought so."

I go inside. It's very bright and I suddenly feel very drunk indeed.

I'm feeling like I did when Tom and Cassidy had a party at their house while their parents were away on holiday. That night, me and Patrick had turned up with the singular musical 'icon' of the early 21st Century, Mr Dane Bowers; or, more accurately, with twenty five metres of bubble wrap stuffed inside a full size all-in-one painting suit with a picture of his face stuck on it.

'Dane' was often a hit at the parties we went to but Patrick and me both lost track of him soon after we arrived. It was one of those nights when things quickly got out of hand; and degenerated to the point where I woke up the next morning, lying next to Cassidy, fully clothed, still wearing my shoes and with little memory of any of the night before or how I'd got there.

After that, the house got cleaned up and we'd taken 'Dane' home. The problem was that none of us remembered when Patrick and me had decided it would be a good idea to drink almost everything out of the medicine cabinet; a small fact that was only discovered after Cassidy and Tom's parents had got home and their mum had gone looking for some cough mixture. The disappearance of most of the cabinet's contents proving impossible to explain without resorting to the truth. It's just a good job their parents seem to like the two of us.

My head's swimming a bit and I know I need to slow the drinking down. I felt ill for days after that night and I think I've learned my lesson. The karaoke's in full swing now and pretty much everyone's sitting around drinking and singing along. The exceptions are Patrick and Cassidy who're just laughing at how pissed Bear has got again and are taking bets on how long after midnight it'll be before he passes out. I know I shouldn't but I can't help joining in. It's half ten now and my guess is he'll be spark out by quarter past twelve. That already looks generous, to be honest.

I get my drink and I'm about to sort out Mary's, when I feel a nudge in my back.

"Where's my drink then Gombrowicz?" Mary asks.

"It's on its way."

"Well hurry it up. It doesn't pay to keep a lady waiting."

"Oh yeah, and what're you going to do about it?"

She pauses and narrows her eyes at me.

"Oh I'll think of something."

We don't go back outside. We sit with the others and for some reason I decide that it's a good idea to sing, '*My Way*'. When I finish, I sit back down and Mary sits on my lap. Patrick's laughing. I look over at him.

"I'm sorry, I'm gonna have to be honest … That was fucking awful mate," he tells me, "But wait till you hear what's coming next."

Mary and me both look round to see our mate Frankie with the microphone in his hand. Patrick isn't wrong. You will never hear 'Yeah' by Usher, droned out quite so horribly in this or any other lifetime. He somehow manages to sing out of time, out of pitch, out of tone and out of key, all at once.

It's a truly epic performance and he's not even drinking. It gets easily the biggest round of applause of the night.

I feel smashed and almost fail to notice Rachel arriving or Mary writing in my notebook. Bear's still standing and has gone outside for a cigarette with Cassidy. I join them, even though I don't smoke. I've always liked passive smoking. I love the flavour and it's a fucking cheap high.

"What's going on with you two tonight?" Bear asks me between drags.

"She's just drunk."

He drops the subject immediately. Too drunk to let conversation get in the way of a smoke.

"Be careful," is all Cassidy adds on the matter.

They go back indoors and Mary comes outside before I can follow them. We sit down, alone in the dark again. She hands me my notebook.

"Don't read what I've written until later," she says.

She looks a little sad. I'm too drunk to really see it.

"What have you put?"

I open the book and she makes no effort to stop me.

My broken and drunken eyes read her words, written in neat handwriting despite how pissed she obviously is:

'I know I shouldn't be saying this but please don't find anyone else.'

Through my numbness I feel the words. It's almost too much.

She looks embarrassed when I look at her again.

"This is still a terrible idea." I tell her even though I know I'm weakening.

"Maybe…"

Then she leans in and kisses me. This time I don't resist. This time I can't.

CHAPTER 17

David was lying on the bed in the blandest, most purely functional room he'd ever been in. A room as antiseptically clean as his father's hospital ward but with less obvious charm. Stark lighting only brought out a bleak sheen to everything in it; the chest of drawers, bedside tables, the TV screen hanging from the wall and the double bed that filled most of the room.

But even in that light, the gloom wouldn't lift from him. There was a knot in his stomach, only inches away from panic. It was only his lack of energy that allowed him to avoid it. He was certain the cloud over his head would pass. It always had done before. He just had to ride it out and look for some kind of distraction.

It was six o' clock, so, he sat up and switched on the television to see the news. There was only more of what he already expected, with the Tory/Lib Dem alliance apparently nearing utter inevitability. He'd already decided it would probably end badly for just about everyone except the people with the most money.

His anger never rose in response. This surprised and irritated him. He thought it might have helped. He glanced over at his suitcase on the floor. Unpacked and unopened because there hadn't seemed like much point if he was only going to be there for a couple of days. When he'd arrived, he booked in until the following Monday, although he had warned the reception staff that he might have to stay for longer.

Gradually, his senses were returning to the dull and empty way he was most used to. Creating an emotional distance was needed after such a long and emotionally draining day. The immediate effect this had though was to make David realise that he hadn't eaten anything since he'd left his flat that morning.

Instantly, his belly started to rumble and he decided to get something to eat. His problem was that he couldn't think of anywhere decent to go. A few years earlier he would have known where a lot of the better restaurants were but his old friend, Norwich, seemed more like a stranger to him than ever before.

His hunger was soon getting worse and he realised that he would have to head out and see what he could find. He'd just turned off the television and was about to have a quick shower, when it suddenly occurred to him that he should have called work to let them know he probably wouldn't be there on Monday.

Although it was all rather dependent on how his dad responded to his treatment, he wasn't planning to rush back. There wasn't much that couldn't be shuffled around for the next week or so. He checked the time again without thinking or realising that he already knew it was too late to call anyone then. He'd have to leave it until Monday morning. He put it out of his head and his stomach rumbled again, almost in annoyance at this latest unnecessary delay.

David stood up just as his phone started ringing. Looking down at the little screen he saw it was Emily calling him. For a moment he was pleased, knowing he could ask what restaurants she'd recommend; then reality kicked in and he realised that she might be calling because she'd heard something from the hospital. The knot in his stomach returned and he answered the phone quickly:

"What is it, what's happened, Emily?"

She seemed to understand what he was thinking straight away.

"Nothing. It's nothing dad. Don't worry, I'm not calling about granddad."

Panic subsided and he was able to speak more calmly:

"Okay, I'm sorry. How are you?"

"I'm fine... Actually, I was just wondering how you were fixed for dinner?"

David could hardly have been happier to hear those words. A smile instantly spread across his face.

"It's funny you should ask that," he said, "I've not actually eaten since I left the flat this morning."

"Then you must come out for a meal with me... There's someone I'd really like you to meet."

He was hardly about to turn down the chance to spend some more time with his daughter or to fill his rumbling stomach.

"That sounds... Well, it sounds great," he told her.

"Thanks dad. Oh and just to let you know that mum's going to be there too. If that's okay."

"Of course. That's fine by me," he said, "Where are we going?"

"Zaks."

David smiled again.

"Mousehold Heath? We haven't been there for years."

"I know."

"That sounds terrific to me, sweetheart."

"It should be," she said, "I'll book the table for half eight and we'll meet you there."

"All right, then. I'll see you soon."

"See you soon dad."

David hung up the phone. Pleased and relatively relaxed, the only negative he could find was the two hour wait to eat. Perhaps because of his hunger and fatigue, his calm didn't last. Negative thoughts crept into his consciousness again. They were about his dad; looping round his mind, he was again gripped by the unshakeable sense that he could have done more to learn about Stanislaw's life before he came to England.

David knew that he really should have gone out to Poland to track down some of his relatives when he'd had the chance. There were gaps to fill in his family history and so many details that were frustratingly hidden away. They were right there, tantalisingly close and still just out of his reach.

Except he realised that it wasn't just his family's history. This story was about Poland and what the country and its people had endured during some of the darkest days in human history. Back when he was a kid and all that information had been right in front of him, he hadn't been looking for it. He hadn't cared. Being half-Polish had no real use to him then. It had just made him feel different to everyone else, when all he wanted was to fit in; to not be the boy in the class with the funny last name that no-one could pronounce.

It was an attitude he would have found forgivable in a child but it hadn't entirely ended in childhood. He'd continued to carry it with him as an adult. In time, he'd learned to appreciate that he was something of a mongrel and that gave him strength. The problem was that he hadn't understood that until it was too late to make any real difference to his life. David's greatest hope was that his kids might be wiser than he was.

He decided he should make himself look presentable for dinner. He shaved and, as he did so, he looked in the mirror. He felt older than he looked although most of his vanity had been left behind by then. The last few years and their self-inflicted wounds had taken their toll.

As he left the room, David realised how nervous he felt. Seeing Melissa earlier had turned out to be fine. The whole situation with his dad had actually made things easier. Dinner that evening was likely to be different because it was a social occasion and he hadn't spent any time like that with Melissa since he'd left her.

He considered cancelling; he could certainly have used his tiredness as a justifiable and almost honest excuse to avoid any awkwardness that night. But he didn't want to be rude. He'd told Emily he'd be there, so he'd be there. Having hardly been the best dad in the world, it was really the least he could do.

Zaks American Diner was too far away for David to walk and was situated on one of the highest hills in Norwich. He headed for his car and once he was on the road he discovered just how much the roads and layout of the traffic lanes had changed since he was last in the city centre.

They weren't the only changes he noticed. St Stephens Street, which had once been the main shopping street in Norwich was very obviously diminished; empty lettings and an excess of bookmakers revealed it to be a shadow of its former glory; completely eclipsed by the shiny, bland, new pull of the city's shopping centres.

After passing a second set of traffic lights that he didn't remember, he swung the car right, up a little hill, past The Bell Hotel. A left-hand turn down then uphill again took him to a red light and a pause in momentum. When he moved again, the clubs and bars along Prince of Wales Road went by quickly; their names looking different although he couldn't remember what they'd been before. He went left along Riverside Road, away from the train station; stealing a brief glance at the River Wensum as it flowed serenely beside the road.

Crossing the roundabout took David up to Mousehold Heath, one of the highest points in Norwich and the place where Robert Kett had based his forces during his rebellion of 1549. It was a revolt that was largely in response to the fencing off of common land by landlords for their own benefit; a classic case of stealing from the poor to give to the rich.

Kett himself had actually been a landowner who disagreed with the practice of Enclosure and offered to lead the rebellion. He and a force of sixteen thousand men even managed to take control of Norwich and defeated a government force sent to suppress the uprising. Within a month it was all over though, when they were defeated by an army led by the Earl of Warwick, and Kett was hung for treason. It was a story that David had learned about at school and had always taken to be a classically British example of glorious failure.

The winding road led up and then flattened out and he saw the sign for *Zaks* on his left. He indicated and turned into the gravel and dirt car park. It hadn't changed. The car park was broadly a circular space with a large green tree at the centre, which had always made parking a little awkward when it was busy. It wasn't too bad that evening. He parked the car facing towards a football pitch and bandstand that was on the other side of the road.

He got out of the car and turned towards a little hill that led up to a black and white hunting lodge, built on two floors that housed the American-style restaurant. It was framed by woodland and, when David looked up through the fading light towards it, he saw Emily, Melissa, and a young man he didn't recognise standing in front.

He briefly hoped the boy was Jonathon. It was soon obvious that he wasn't. They both had dark hair but this boy was taller and less stocky than his son and as David got closer he could see that Emily was holding his hand.

"Hello," he said to the three of them, as he got to the top of the hill.

"Hi dad," Emily replied.

She went to him and gave him a hug. She turned to the young man.

"Dad, this is my boyfriend, Oliver."

Oliver held out his hand to David.

"Hello Mr Gombrowicz, it's nice to meet you."

David took his hand, shook it and smiled. He could tell that he was nervous.

"Nice to meet you too."

"Shall we go inside? It's getting a bit parky out here," Melissa enquired.

"Absolutely!" David announced with sudden positivity, "I'm bloody starving."

He stood back and let them lead the way inside. Once the door swung shut behind him, he discovered that it was significantly darker than the evening outside. Classic posters and adverts from the 50s, 60s and 70s covered the walls, just as he remembered; and various songs from that period played loud enough to hear but not too loud to have drowned out any conversation. A pretty blonde waitress showed them to their table.

It was soon obvious to David that Oliver was rather a quiet lad. He seemed pleasant though and that was enough. He'd realised years before then that it didn't particularly matter what he thought of Emily's boyfriends. All that mattered was that they treated her well and that they were happy together. If she was with someone he found tolerable to be around it was just a bonus. He didn't have to love this boy; he just had to accept it if Emily did.

There wasn't too much doubt about his daughter's feelings or that Oliver felt much the same way towards her. It was visual and verbal. Looks and words, compliments and touching hands. And David was simply relieved and pleased to see her so happy.

They ordered their food and, to his relief, it arrived soon after. He had to stop himself eating his Rockhouse burger and potato wedges too quickly. Indigestion would have been inevitable. He savoured the first mouthful and there was a lull in conversation until Melissa had finished the first of her Surf'n'Turf burger.

"Do you remember the first time Emily saw the sea?" she asked David.

"How could I forget?" he replied, with a grin.

Emily knew what was coming.

"Oh God!" she said.

Oliver put his hand on hers and smiled as David started to tell the story:

"We were in…"

"Dorset," Melissa said looking at David and then at Oliver, "We always went to Dorset. Lovely part of the world."

"It was…Lyme Regis that time?" David asked.

"That's right."

"We went to the beach and Emily was what? Two or three? And she was terribly over excited to be going to the seaside. In fact, she was so excited that when we got onto the beach she started running as fast as she could towards the sea. She was like a little Speedy Gonzalez but the tide was out and we thought she'd slow down but she didn't. She just kept going on and on and on. Until I ended up having to leg it after her to make sure she didn't run all the way into the water."

"You were a mad child!" Melissa told her and then looked at Oliver again, "And I still remember having to dress her up for school every day as whatever character from the telly or films she wanted to be. She was Supergirl once and Madonna, of all people."

"Yeah, well, Jon was worse than me," Emily declared, defending herself, "Spiderman, Indiana Jones, Bruce Springsteen, even Stevie Wonder."

"Christ!" said Oliver.

"I know," David told him, "Honestly, I blame the parents!"

He looked at Melissa with a grin on his face. She smiled back with genuine warmth; her face completely relaxed in the synthetic candle light.

"Definitely," she agreed.

Emily just shrugged and looked at Oliver. He gently laid his hand back onto hers. David's smile beamed again. He didn't doubt that his daughter's precious heart was in safe hands.

He was so hungry that evening that he easily managed to finish all his food and, with his belly full, David enjoyed the evening a great deal. He'd always liked telling stories, especially when he was able to relax with the people around him. It had also been a long time since he'd been able to reminisce about things like holidays or all the family's little in-jokes from when the children had been little.

Even so, something was missing. He wished that Jonathon was there. He missed him. Or more honestly, he missed the little boy who used to look up to him and who'd loved him just because he happened to be his dad.

It seemed like so much time had passed since he'd watched him play football every Sunday. That had been for seven or eight years and back then Jonathon had wanted to be a professional footballer. He'd been a good little player too and David had thought it was possible that he might make a career out of it; hoping that one day he might even have got the chance to wear the yellow and green of Norwich City.

In fact, by the time he was sixteen Jonathon had given it up because he'd lost interest in it. That had become a pattern he'd repeated on plenty of occasions since. He would get interested in something, become good at it and then get bored and move onto something else.

As he'd got older, David had found that deeply frustrating, although he never really made any effort to understand why. He'd just got annoyed instead. That had been a mistake and by then he knew it. He should have handled it differently. He should have kept calm and let his boy live his own life. Perhaps if he had, it would have been more difficult for Jonathon to cut him out of his life so fully.

After paying the bill, the four of them walked out of the restaurant and David found himself detached, his thoughts increasingly dominated by his father and his son. He hoped there was still a chance to make things right with both of them. Unfortunately, as he walked down the hill, through the dark and towards his car, he couldn't help thinking that it might already be too late.

CHAPTER 18

Karski understood that the liquid had blinded him and he still couldn't move. He could also tell that he wasn't in the train yard anymore. He was on a train. It was obvious from the sound and the feeling of movement around him. Unfortunately, that was all he could really be sure about.

Despite his body still being constrained by something still unknown to him, his mind remained free to travel wherever it wished. It soon took him out of the train and into the sky; flying over Pileck's criss-crossing train lines; the steam from the trains and smoke from burning towns and villages rising up to create another layer of mist and vagueness over the land.

He floated through it to another train that was moving in the opposite direction to the one containing his body. Inside that train and along the entire length of it were hundreds of Pilecki, crushed and crowded in. And there, hidden with all those frightened people was the only man who wanted and needed to be there. Witold was just another face in the crowd but Karski was pleased simply to know he was still alive and had a chance of completing his mission. There was still hope that Salamander's sacrifice would not be in vain.

Witold's face soon faded from Karski's mind, instantly replaced by another that he thought he recognised. It looked like the face he had seen reflected in the lake in Tarek Nor forest except that this time something was different about it. The man's hair was a lot longer and he was clean shaven. He looked slightly older and was playing in a garden with his two young children, a girl and a boy. Something told Karski that he knew them too although there was nothing else in his mind or memory to back that up; emptiness remained and nothing more was revealed to him.

The sun shone on a bright and clear day that was unlike any he had seen since he had been in Pileck. The man and his children looked happy together; the happy family image warming Karski's heart even though he couldn't be sure why. Somehow it just seemed like it was the true heart of all that he was and all that he could be.

When that image faded, he was left in foggy darkness. Back in the sky, he looked down upon a city that he soon realised was Vistula. On either side of it, two huge armies had gathered to face each other.

On one side was the fearsome army of the winged Sinistrians. Thousands of them were arranged in lines, on the ground outside the city. Every one of them had a machine gun, rifle or pistol drawn, ready to attack. At the back of these lines was the larger weaponry, like mortars and grenade launchers; while in the air, there were thousands more heavily armed Sinistrian soldiers, carrying flame throwers, grenades and more rifles and machine guns.

Karski flew to the other side of the city to take a closer look at an even larger army that was gathered there; just across the river that ran beside Vistula. There were many thousands of men. They were powerful and heavily armed with very similar weapons to the Sinistrians. These were not normal men like the Pilecki though. This was the Curzonian army and the Curzonian's were shape shifters; giant spiders that could also take the form of men. There were hundreds of thousands of huge, venomous spiders standing alongside what looked like normal soldiers and they were all waiting for the battle to begin.

Next, his mind showed him a vision of Vistula itself; the passage of days and weeks, going by in an instant. The uprising in Vistula began with the Pilecki taking up their weapons against the Sinistrians inside the city. The soldiers were not dressed to look like civilians; they were dressed in army uniforms, with the red and white armbands that represented Pileck clearly visible. They took the Sinistrians by surprise and managed to take control of large parts of the city. For a brief time, even City hall was under their control.

It couldn't last. The Sinistrian's gradually took control and Vistula became a mess of upturned paving slabs, roads disintegrated by mortar fire and bullet holes in walls. The fire and ashes of homes became no more than burned out shells, as entire blocks of the city were levelled by the Sinistrian firepower.

The Pilecki held on, waiting for help from The Alliance or the Curzonians. It never arrived but they didn't stop fighting. Their bravery was extraordinary as they fought for the city that was being stolen from them, house by house and beautiful building by beautiful building. It was a fight and battle they were destined to lose and Karski knew then that he was seeing the future,

His thoughts faded once again. He felt better when the brightness of day returned and he was shown the image of a beautiful young woman with long dark hair. Her skin was pale and she was wearing a red dress with a white flower pattern. He watched as she stood on a bridge looking down towards him. She was the most beautiful woman Karski had ever seen in his life. He watched her smile at him and he felt like he'd found his home again.

Then it was over. She was gone and the light and the visions in his mind were too. All that remained was darkness and all he could do was listen. He could hear the sound of the train's engine much more clearly than before. The roar was louder and he could feel that the train was moving faster. He wondered where the Sinistrians were taking him.

Then he tried not to think about it. He was sure that it wouldn't be anywhere he'd ever want to be. Witold had already said that they thought he was some kind of terrible and hideous weapon and it seemed obvious that they would try to make him turn on his own people; to break him in some way and make him into something that was as awful as they were. He recalled the emptiness around the fire in their eyes and knew he couldn't let that happen. He had to stay true to himself, to his home, and to his family.

The thought made him feel strong until another vision appeared in his mind. Under blinding surgical lights, he saw himself tied down as a masked man took a scalpel and cut his wrists open. Karski felt the intensity of the pain and then the way it deadened until it was neither numbness nor the excruciating horror he was expecting either. He looked down and saw his opened veins and the blood pouring from his body. The eyes of the masked man were wild and sadistically frenzied and he could tell he was taking the utmost pleasure in everything he was doing.

Sick with horror at what he saw in his mind, he fought to shut the vision out. It worked but only briefly. The dark deathly liquid loosened its grip upon him and his sight returned. It still wasn't very clear. It looked like the night had been lit up like the Deep Amnios; like blinking lights in the darkness. Colours floated down to show that he was sitting in the carriage of a train surrounded by twenty dark angels of death.

The noise of the engine grew even louder. Despite this though, he was suddenly aware that other sounds were growing more prominent. It was the sound of bombs that were falling and exploding all around the train. Some of them sounded like they were a long way away, while others sounded like they were very close to hitting the train. Each time there was a near miss the speed of the train increased even more and Karski wondered if they were being bombed by the Alliance, the Curzonians, or a combination of the two. Whichever it was, the Sinistrians in the carriage were becoming increasingly restless. They were stuck on the train and knew that if there was a direct hit there was little chance of escape.

Even so, they were still a frightening and intimidating sight. Machine guns and rifles were held at the ready as they sat, and the cold fire in their eyes remained completely trained upon his paralysed body.

By then, Karski's fear was pressing down upon him where he sat. There seemed to be no way out. Alone in some kind of hell, it seemed that even if he could free himself from the liquid imprisoning him, there would be no way to escape the Sinistrians or the bombs still falling on the ground outside.

Hope appeared to evaporate and the deathlike stench of the black liquid coated and completely blinded him again. He realised then that it was a liquid that was the opposite of the Deep Amnios. Everything about it was emptiness; more like the dark end of a street; like the depths of space or even the dark era that would herald the end of the known universe.

In that darkness, he listened to the sound of bombs exploding; close enough to almost be able to hear the vibrations. The sound repeated and regular; one explosion following another, a metronome with every impact, like the dripping of a tap or the ticking of the grandfather clock Karski suddenly saw inside his mind. The clock that stood in the hallway of his family's home in Vistula. He was searching through the house, looking for somewhere to hide. He looked in cabinets, cupboards, under the stairs, and behind doors. There was nowhere and this wasn't a child's game either. It was life and death. He was looking for gaps between walls or under the floorboards; anywhere that might help him escape. It was already too late. A huge spider swung from a web, through a window near to where he stood. The Curzonian shape shifter immediately changed into a man, pulled out a gun and shot him in the head.

The darkness returned and he only heard the sound of one more bomb before another smashed into the train and blew it up. The sound of metal buckling and further explosions eventually giving way to stillness and silence. For several moments, he genuinely believed that it was the end. But that was when a vision of the future returned to his mind; a single moving image of the wild, evil sadistic eyes of the man in the mask; the doctor he knew would inflict the most horrific surgery upon his body.

There was no mistaking the truth. Karski knew that this was the way the Sinistrians would try to break him. He knew he could cope with that knowledge. At the same time though, the thought of what it would mean if they were successful made the fear he had been trying to suppress rise up through him until it became the only thing he was still able to feel.

CHAPTER 19

We're on our own outside for quite a while just kissing. It's good. My hands are on her arse over her jeans and I move my face away to stare at hers; drinking it in because the starlight suits the sweetness of her smile. Eventually, she steps away.

"I need the loo," she says.

I watch her go. She glances back at me, showing off her big eyes and long limbs; like a sexy Bambi. Then she grins, looks away and walks inside. I decide not to stay where I am and go in too. Everyone else has left us to it. It's after midnight and Bear has passed out on the kitchen floor and everyone else has gone into the living room to watch a film. I stay in the kitchen waiting for Mary to come back and Patrick nips in to get himself another beer.

"You all right?" he asks, with a ridiculous fucking smirk on his face.

I try to play it cool.

"Yeah, not bad," I say and manage to look a complete dick.

"I bet," he declares, still smirking.

Mary walks in.

"See you two later then," he says and goes back into the living room.

She walks up to me and kisses me again. I think I might be starting to sober up a bit and I stop her.

"What are we doing?" I ask.

"Well, I'm doing what I wanted to do yesterday."

She leans in and puts her lips to mine again. It's difficult to fight it. I try anyway.

"So this was all planned?" I ask.

"Maybe a little bit."

"Well, I can't say I expected to be doing this with you tonight."

"I did," she tells me and we're all over each other again.

I know I ought to stop this even though I really don't want to.

"You know, it would probably be best to sober up and see how things look in the morning."

"You're probably right," she says, "But that would mean I've worn this ridiculous pair of knickers for nothing."

She turns away from me, undoes her jeans and pulls them down just enough to show off the white cotton underwear that's disappearing between her bum cheeks. It's quite an image and she quickly does up her jeans, turns and kisses me. It's a ridiculously intense and sexy kiss, and I apparently have no willpower. There's suddenly no doubt what we both want. She stops and looks in my eyes.

"Are you going to take me home then?" she asks.

"My place or yours?"

"Mine's nearer but we'll have to be quiet because everyone's there."

We leave without saying goodbye to anyone. I doubt they'll be surprised. They had to know what was going to happen. It's nearly one in the morning and it's a bit chilly. More kissing keeps me warm, although a part of me worries that she'll have sobered up enough by the time we get to hers to think better of the idea.

I stare into her eyes and tell her, "I've missed this".

"So have I."

Another kiss follows. And this one is just overwhelmingly passionate and I want her more than any woman I've ever wanted in my life. I even tell her so.

"Patience, darling boy," she says with a smile and a giggle.

We walk on and I remember the time that we walked together from my place to hers; about five miles with her barefoot for most of it too and I still don't know why. I do remember giving her a piggy back at one point, when we went over a load of gravel on the pavement. She was worried she weighed too much. The truth is I've always thought she was just about perfect.

There are no piggy backs this time and we're soon at her house. We kiss on the doorstep and I almost expect her to tell me to go home and call her tomorrow. She doesn't. Instead, she walks in grabs my hand, and pulls me into the house.

We're quiet, trying not to wake her mum and dad, or her sister. I notice nothing but her as we go into the kitchen.

"Would you like a drink," she whispers.

"No I'm all right," I reply.

"Good."

This kiss quickly spirals. I love the taste of her mouth more than almost anything. Our hands are everywhere and she's lying back against the kitchen table.

"You'd better get me into that bedroom quick," she tells me, standing up and pushing me away.

She leaves the kitchen and goes along the hallway and I follow, transfixed as she starts taking her clothes off and depositing them on the floor. First her red top, then almost instantaneously, her bra. Her jeans are halfway off when she gets to her bedroom door and opens it to me. I grab her. Our lips meet and we almost fall into the room.

The rest of her clothes are soon off and so are mine. We have sex on her floor a couple of times. At one point she's on top and realises how noisy she's being. Her sister's in the next room. She bites her lip and keeps on going.

We lay on the floor afterwards, limbs entangled. Mary seems happy, which is all I ever want for her. Then she gets up quickly and goes out into the hall to pick up the clothes she left there. I watch her wonderful nakedness go, come back and lock the door behind her again. She pulls the duvet off her bed and puts it over and around us as she snuggles up to me.

"Are you all right," I ask her.

"Yes definitely," she says with another quick kiss.

It's quiet for a few moments and I wonder what she's thinking. Then she asks:

"You aren't going to write about me, are you?"

"Only if you hurt me."

I say it with a grin but immediately regret it.

"Sorry, I didn't mean it like that Maz. I'm still pretty drunk."

"It's okay," she says and I kind of know it isn't really.

She cuddles up to me for a while. I can see she's getting tired. It's a quarter to four already.

"I should probably go," I tell her.

"Yeah, I need my beauty sleep," she says.

I laugh. She couldn't be more wrong. I get dressed and she puts a baggy t-shirt on to walk me to the front door.

Kissing on the doorstep, my hands are on her soft, bare bum. I'm very tempted to go back inside and fuck her again. You never can tell if you'll ever get another chance with Mary. I manage to resist the urge though.

"I love you," I whisper to her instead.

"I love you too. Goodnight."

"Night."

I watch her close the door, and then I turn and walk away. There's a haze of something unreal that I notice and I suddenly feel really tired. It's probably just knowing that I've got five miles to walk. I wish I could've stayed with her. I hadn't noticed just how cold it was when we were walking to her house. Now it feels bloody freezing.

It's best that I just keep moving. It's slightly more uphill heading back but at least it gets my blood pumping again. The booze is clearing from my head and thoughts start to appear. It's the first time I've had some time to myself in days. That's not necessarily a good thing though. I usually miss too much when I stop to think.

I start wondering if tonight was really such a good idea. What if she can't deal with it and disappears for months again? As good as it was tonight, it definitely won't have been worth it if she does.

I mean, I'm not completely stupid. I know she's gonna go sooner or later. You can't exactly fast track an acting career in Norfolk. I could always go with her. But I probably won't.

Maybe we're better off just being friends anyway. But even when that's all we were I always wanted more. I can't help it. I can't help myself. She's the most beautiful woman I've ever known and she could probably kill me and make me like it.

Maybe it's because she's different to me. She's sort of more like Patrick than I am. You see, they're both fireworks; he's a Roman Candle and she's a Catherine Wheel; and both of them are burning, burning, burning, so bright and wild; the wildest of all the lights that colour my life and my nights. But can that last forever or will they be gone when the sun comes up?

I try not to think about any of that but they've become the only things on my mind; looping round endlessly, mercilessly until I reach into the inside pocket of my jacket, find my earphones and attach them to my phone. I look through the dark and into the bright little screen and try to decide what to listen to. I almost go for Destroyer until I see The Mars Volta. I have a strange urge for some *'De-loused in the Comatorium'*.

I love the noise; A bit of prog punk with a whole load of unusual shapes. It manages to take my mind somewhere else when I walk through the centre of Harleston. Then I think about my granddad and feel bad. I shouldn't have left the hospital the way I did and I should have gone to see him a whole lot more after nanny died. I left it up to Emily. She's the good one. I'm the evil fucking child.

And. Fuck it, I really need to pee. I've been putting it off and now I can really feel it. I think about going back to Joey's but I figure they'll all be well asleep by now. Getting home, as quickly as I can is my only option. I speed up and soon cross the Redenhall roundabout. 'Keep walking and don't let up,' I tell myself.

Another mile in about fifteen minutes and I run up my drive. I find my keys and run inside, straight to the toilet. What a relief. What a fucking amazing relief! I actually laugh at how good it feels.

It's just before quarter past five. I decide to do a bit of writing before I call it a night. As soon as I make that decision though, I feel really tired so I lay down on my bed. I pull my clothes off quickly and almost immediately I don't feel or think anything anymore.

CHAPTER 20

David opened the car door to Melissa, letting her in before he got in himself. He was relieved she was there. When he'd offered her a lift back it was only partly because he had thought it would be easier for Emily and Oliver. In truth, he simply didn't want to be left alone.

Once he was inside the car, the briefest glance only confirmed that Melissa looked much the same as she did on the day they had met. For a moment David wished he was eighteen again. He thought everything had been so much simpler then. People had often trotted out the cliché that "Youth was wasted on the young". By that point in his life, he'd decided that he knew what they meant.

"Are you all right?" Melissa suddenly asked him.

"Yes," he said.

"No, David I mean it… Are you really all right? You played it well in there… Em was worried it was all a bit inappropriate to introduce you to Oliver when Stan's so unwell and everything. But…"

He took a deep breath and hoped for an end to the conversation.

"When else would she have got the opportunity?"

He hoped that might be enough for her to drop the subject. It wasn't.

"That's what I thought," she continued, "So are you all right? I know Em doesn't want to see it but this is affecting you quite badly isn't it?"

She looked concerned and he wished that she didn't.

"I'm fine Mel. It's just been a hard couple of days."

He started the engine of the car, hoping the sound would drown out any more conversation. It worked up to a point, and he was able to drive through the city without many more words being spoken. What he noticed though was that the look of concern on Melissa's face didn't change. She kept glancing over; checking on him. By the third time she did it, he found it quite touching. The familiar feeling of self-loathing followed soon after.

He drove the car into the driveway of the house that the two of them had shared for nearly twenty-five years. For a long time he'd wondered why she hadn't moved after he'd left. His assumption at the time was that the memories of their life there would have been painful to relive on a daily basis. He'd never asked her why she decided to stay though, and by then it was really none of his business anyway.

"Thanks for the lift David. Would you like to come in for a drink?" she asked, kindly.

The offer took him by surprise but he didn't want to refuse. He still had no desire to be on his own.

"Thanks that'd be lovely," he replied.

She unlocked the door and walked in. He followed her. The house wasn't quite how he remembered it. She'd certainly had a lot of decorating done, with the paintwork, walls and the carpets all completely different and definitely improved by being lighter and fresher. Despite this, it still remained close enough to his memory of it to make him feel like a ghost haunted by the spectre of a home and a life that was long gone.

"The place looks great," he told her, "Even better than I remember."

"Thanks."

She looked pleased and then quickly and seamlessly shifted into hostess mode.

"Now what can I get you to drink? Tea? Coffee?"

"A cup of tea would be great."

"Then a cup of tea it shall be," she said with a gentle smile.

She walked into the kitchen and he followed her, looking closely at the interiors of the house as he went.

The word "Wow!" slipped from his mouth as he stepped into the kitchen after her.

The oven was a big and beautiful green machine with brass handles and a gas hob. The cupboards, fixtures and fittings were all coordinated with each other and all of Melissa's utensils, pots and pans were within easy reach. It was practical yet stylish and homely; a mirror image of the lady of the house. For David, it was like something out of a dream.

"Well, you know that I always said it was the most important room in the house," Melissa told him, "So I had to make sure it was perfectly designed for me to make use of."

He sat down at the kitchen table as she made the tea. While it brewed she sat down opposite him.

"I still don't think you're quite right David," she suddenly said to him.

This time though he lacked the strength or energy to argue.

"All right... Yes... The thing with Stan. With dad... It's hit me a lot harder than I thought... I'd put all that stuff away. And I just didn't think about him unless I had to... And most of the thoughts I had about him weren't exactly positive."

"I think I can understand that."

"But that's the worst part because I think I was completely wrong... I said some absolutely terrible things about the awkward old sod and I'm not sure he deserved any of them."

"I don't know. He definitely is an awkward old sod."

"But that's just him. It's his manner... I sure as hell wouldn't want to only be judged on... Well, to be honest, I wouldn't really want to be judged on most of the things I've done in my life."

For an instant there was surprise and then a smile appeared on Melissa's face.

"Bloody hell!" she said, "Is that self-awareness I spy in Mr David Gombrowicz?"

"It's about bloody time isn't it?"

There was no lightness in his tone, only bitter knowledge.

"Well, I didn't want to say…" she said, raising her eyebrows.

When he didn't respond she spoke more seriously again:

"I'm sorry, I'm teasing David… Look, we both know you had your reasons for feeling that way about your dad… That's just the way things are sometimes in families… You were hurt and he was always a good person to blame."

"Yeah. I think that's the worst part. It was too easy for me to do that… And then I went the other way and I… Well, I ended up getting too caught up in what I wanted. I wanted to know more about him. I wanted to understand him and I just don't think he wanted to burden anyone with all the things he went through… I was stupid enough to resent that… Now I'm thinking that… Oh, I don't know. Maybe it made the Alzheimer's a bit of a relief to him… If it did, I honestly think he'd earned it."

She didn't say a word for a few seconds and just looked at him.

"David Gombrowicz, I really didn't think you could still find any way to shock me after all these years but you've managed it twice tonight."

"I just… I feel so angry with myself for not looking closer. For not having any kind of fucking empathy. And now it's probably too late to even try making it up to him. And he wouldn't even have a bloody clue why I'd need to."

"Stop that!" she said sharply, her eyes were wide and serious, "You're his son. I'm absolutely certain that somewhere deep down, underneath the haze, he still loves you."

Self-pity appeared at that point and David couldn't help giving in to it.

"It feels like he's just about all I've got left Mel."

When the tears fell from his eyes then, David realised that they'd been trying to do so for almost the entire day. Melissa went to him and put a gently consoling arm around his shoulders. That was the limit of any pandering to his self-pity that she would be involved in though.

"You're wrong." she told him bluntly, "You have Emily and Jonathon too."

"Of course, I know that. But Jonathon's…"

"Jonathon's what? Don't be a fool David… He's your son and he's a good boy."

"I know that Mel. I just feel like I've lost him."

"Well you're wrong again…He's just like you, you know," she said.

"Really?"

"You're surprised?" she asked, "He's hardly the first Gombrowicz who didn't really get on with his father."

"I suppose not… Do you know if he's still friends with that Anders boy?" he asked.

"I take it that you're not a fan then."

"It's not that."

"Except that it is, isn't it," she said, cutting through his all too obvious lie.

He smiled. She had become painfully good at doing that with him.

"All right maybe it is a bit".

They both knew that was an understatement. David considered Patrick Anders to be a thoroughly negative influence upon Jonathon. One that was likely to lead him into a lot of trouble. It was the kind of thinking that managed to both elevate and undervalue Jonathon and Patrick equally.

"Yes they're still friends," Melissa told him with a shrug, "Look, Patrick's no angel but it's not like he's a criminal... Besides, Jon trusts him and I honestly don't see why he wouldn't. He looks out for him... Personally, I like that and I think you should too."

He looked at her. She was defending their boy again and he hated to admit that she might know better than he did on the matter. He said nothing.

She stood up and turned away from him. She went to the work surface and poured out the tea into two matching blue mugs. She added milk to both of them, and sugar only to the mug that she handed to David after giving the tea a quick stir. Once she had gone back to fetch her own, she sat back on the chair opposite him.

David sipped his tea. It was hot but good. It was another thing that made Melissa so great in difficult circumstances; the ability to make a decent cup of tea in those situations shouldn't ever be underestimated.

"Jonathon's certainly lucky to have you to defend him," he eventually said to her.

She put her tea down on the table and fixed him firmly with her gaze.

"And I think you know as well as anyone that it's just something that mums do."

He nodded, smiled and then sighed. There was too much understanding, too much love, and too much sadness to do much else.

"When did you get so wise, Mel?" he asked.

"Why did you never notice before?" she replied.

Her words stung. He didn't wince and nodded his head instead.

"I really am sorry, Mel," he said to her.

"What for? That?"

She shrugged her shoulders; trying to ignore the more obvious answer.

"No, well yes. But really for... Well, you know. Everything else."

Her face was serene but serious as she sighed out her response

"And I was doing such a good job of pretending it never happened."

"Yeah..."

"Look, I think we're both a bit too old for screaming and shouting about it."

"I should have grown up," he said.

"You're probably right," she told him, "But you aren't exactly the first man not to manage it."

David felt ashamed of himself as he realised that he truly loved Melissa. It wasn't a great passionate love that might fracture and distort a soul or a life; it was more calm, more generous, more real and honest than that. It was a love built on the simple and inescapable understanding that he was lucky to have known her at all; and a recognition of so many of the things he'd failed to appreciate when they'd actually been a couple.

"I'd like to try to find some way of making things up to you…At least a little bit."

"You can't and I can't let you," she told him, flatly, "What you can do is try to be a better dad. They both deserve that… And especially Jonathon."

He nodded his head. She was right. So, he responded by telling her the most honest thing he could think of at that moment:

"I'm glad you were the mother of our children, Mel."

"Well, I'm glad I was too…"

For David there was some reassurance in those words. Part of him had always hated the idea of Melissa hating him. While he wasn't stupid enough to believe she hadn't ever despised him, the last few hours made him think that perhaps the years had dulled her anger at least a little bit.

"You should probably move back out this way," she said, "All the family you've got left are out here anyway… And you're hardly getting any younger."

"Thanks," he said, sarcastically.

"Well you aren't. None of us are. And you're miles out of the way in Alveston."

"It's only a few hours' drive," he tried to explain.

"Yes, and how often have you made that journey in the last couple of years?"

"All right that's true enough but I have work and I haven't always felt very welcome round here."

"And whose fault is that?" she asked, with a broad grin.

It was playful enough to not really seem like they were arguing although it was hardly a fair fight anyway. David had no comeback at all. Looking at her, part of him wanted to be annoyed at what she was saying. He wanted to justify himself; perhaps even suggest he was simply a victim of the circumstances. But he couldn't and instead, he said nothing and let her go on:

"I'm sure that if you were here, showing your face on a regular basis, you'd soon wear Jonathon down… Like I said, he's a lot like you. And if you were serious earlier about wishing you'd learned more about Stan then he could probably tell you quite a lot."

"Really? How?" David asked.

"Just after your mum died, he started looking into Stan's life in Poland. He managed to find out quite a lot too... Even though the majority of the records from that time were lost or destroyed during the war, it still sounded like there was enough to turn it into a good book..."

David was surprised. He would never have guessed that Jonathon had any interest in his family's history.

"I should probably talk to him," he said.

"I'd have thought that goes without saying".

"Yes, I suppose it does really," he agreed

The smile that appeared on his face was subdued and she offered a similar one in return. At that moment, things were completely calm and he was glad about that. It felt like they were old friends, who just happened to have a rather chequered past. David genuinely hoped that this would be how it stayed.

He took a quick look at his watch and saw that it was nearly half past eleven.

"I should probably get going," he said.

"All right," she replied, standing up.

He finished the last of his tea.

"I have to say that, amazingly, I've had a very nice evening David."

"So have I."

They walked to the front door and she opened it. David stepped outside and immediately turned to face her.

"You are happy aren't you Mel?" he asked, suddenly.

It was a question that he was almost as surprised to hear as she was.

Melissa paused to think. He looked into her eyes and knew her answer before she spoke again:

"Aside from the last twenty four hours or so, I can honestly say that my life is everything I could wish for right now."

"Then I'm happy to hear that."

"Thank you."

They opened their arms and gave each other a warm hug. Then David gave her a tender kiss on the cheek, turned away and got into his car. Melissa closed the door and he sat for a moment in silence looking at the house. He smiled and nodded to himself, then he started the engine and drove away.

CHAPTER 21

"Hello Mr Karski," an unseen voice said to him, "I am Doctor Eugenius Stark and I am here to take care of you."

Karski was still blind and the all-consuming darkness made Stark's voice seem more powerful and imposing:

"You have been involved in a train accident and it will require my particular expertise to fix you and make you strong again."

Karski tried to move his arms and legs but he was completely immobilised. His lack of freedom was different to how it had been on the train though. He could feel the straps on his limbs that were fixing him to what he assumed was some kind of table.

"Do not struggle Mr Karski. This treatment is for your own good and for the good of us all."

He struggled some more and tried to speak but he felt several strong hands on his throat, holding him down and strangling his words. He relented. The hands did not.

"You cannot comprehend what you can become. And that is your biggest problem Mr Karski. Without my help, you lack the imagination to be everything that you can possibly be. Without me, you cannot become The Manterrosh, the scourge of the Curzonian menace. It is that which is your true destiny."

Karski tried to protest. It was no good though, he couldn't make a sound.

"You and your people are nothing more than caterpillars. You are insects that do nothing other than exist. The rest of your insignificant species will never be able to attain the extraordinary greatness that I and I alone can give to you. They will never ever become butterflies. They will only be destroyed... But you can still be saved. You can join with us to become the most feared of all the weapons our glorious leader has at his disposal. Then the world will belong to Erom Babylon and the great Sinistrian people. And you will be a part of that too; another glorious instrument of our greatness and the defining example of my artistry."

The voice stopped and the hands left Karski's throat. Everything was silent, black and empty and he wondered what Stark was waiting for. He felt his hands and legs being released and hope briefly swelled in his chest. He wondered if he was being rescued and freed from his dark prison. He didn't have to wonder for long. Before he could react in any way, his neck was being strapped down onto the table.

"I want to give you a sporting chance," he heard the doctor say.

Karski recognised the next thing he felt. There was pain in his wrists and he knew they were being cut and his veins were being opened. He felt the same burning pain in his feet and then his legs and arms were strapped down onto the table again.

The vision of his torture appeared clearly in his mind. Removed from the action, looking down from above, he saw that Doctor Stark was a huge and imposing Sinistrian. His black wings were obscured by a white coat and a white mask was covering the lower half of his face. What was still visible was the fire in his eyes, filled with sickening and murderous intent.

All Karski could do was watch as Stark took a huge butcher knife in his hand and started to speak words in a language that he didn't recognise or understand:

"Hanc igitur oblationem servitutis nostrae, sed et cunctae familiae tuae quaesumnus Domine, ut placates accipias, diesque nostros in tua pace disponas, atque ab aeterna damnatione nos eripi, et in electorum tuorum jubeas grege numerari."

The Doctor joined his hands together around the handle of the knife, held it above his head and plunged it into Karski's torso.

With horribly vivid clarity, Karski saw his own live dissection. An excruciating burning sensation moved all the way down his chest while his blood spilled out all over the room. His heart was still beating as it was exposed to him, along with the rest of his organs. Doctor Stark spoke again:

"Supra quae propitio ac seron vulto respicere digneris:et accepta habere, sicuti accepta habere dignatus es munera pueri tui justi Abel, et sacrificium patriarchae nostril Abrahae, et quod tibi obtulit summus sacerdos tuus Melchisedech sanctum sacrificium immaculatam hostiam."

The pain began to subside. There was clearly more to this indecent treatment of his body than simple torture. The straps were removed from his limbs and neck but Karski was too weak to offer any resistance. More blood flowed as he was flipped over onto his front on the table. The burning sensation spread to his upper back as Doctor Stark disintegrated his shoulder blades with his knife.

The fire in the Sinistrian doctor's eyes burned bright red and wild with the pleasure he took in his work. The linen mask covering his face becoming drenched in blood, as flesh was ripped from the body on the slab.

"Hostiam, puram hostam, sanctam hostiam, immaculatam," Stark bellowed, as his face was further obscured by the blood of destruction and creation.

He went on sculpting his grotesque masterpiece until all that appeared to be left of Karski was a mind that could do nothing more than look at the Doctor's handiwork. And it was that, which was the real torture, the real sacrifice he had to endure. He could do nothing to stop what the Doctor would make him into. All he could be sure of was that he would be a truly terrible and terrifying creature.

Doctor Stark knew exactly what he was making; creating from the raw materials of Pilecki flesh, weaponry, machinery and evil. Karski was being twisted and distorted to be made immense; to be made into a machine of death; an instrument of torture for anyone who tried to fight it. The Manterrosh: The single greatest weapon of that or any other war.

PART 3

CHAPTER 22

I'm surprised by how early it is when I wake up. I don't feel too bad either. Thought I'd be a lot more hungover than I actually am.

I have a quick shower, get dressed and think about writing. I'm ready, with ideas bubbling just beneath the surface. I get the laptop out and hear a knock on the front door. Patrick's arrived just in time to give me another excuse not to do any work.

He seems to be in a good mood.

"How are you this morning?" he asks me.

"Not too bad really. What did I miss after I left last night?"

"We were watching 'Evil Dead' when you two fucked off. Is she here now, by the way? I can go if you want."

"No, I walked her back to hers," I tell him.

"Oh… I'm so proud of you, ya big love machine."

I hate it when he does this. I shake my head and he decides not to push it.

"How'd you get here so early anyway?" I ask, "You didn't walk did you?"

"Nah, I got a lift with Bear, he was taking Cassidy back to Norwich this morning."

"Oh right, fair enough."

One of the best things about Patrick is that even though he's a completely open book with me, he actually lets me say as much or as little as I'm comfortable with. If it'd been him that copped off with a fit girl last night, he would've already been sharing way more information than I really wanted to know by now. And he'd probably exaggerate a whole heap of details too. I know he does that because he likes me to laugh at him and the things he does. I'd laugh anyway. He's the funniest person I've ever met.

That's one of the reasons why he's also like a safety valve to me. He stops me getting too stuck inside my own head. I just can't manage to be all that stressed when I'm around him. It's been the same ever since we met.

He was Cassidy's friend first. And she sort of introduced us at the Wortwell Bell one night. He made quite an impression. By half ten that night he was challenging anyone who went into the gents to a competition to see who could throw up the most. He was sure he couldn't lose but no-one bothered to take up the challenge anyway. At the end of the night, he staggered outside, fell down onto the pavement, made a brief attempt to crawl the three miles to Harleston; before lying flat out on his back and calling his dad to pick him up and take him home.

The thing is though, that wasn't actually the night we met at all. It was years before then and I didn't even realise. I was sitting on top of a roof at three in the morning. A group of us had climbed over the High School gates and wandered around the grounds of the school for a while. We soon got bored and tried looking at the places we never got to see when we were students there. We ended up on the roof of the art block, just sitting down and looking out over the playing field, as a thick fog covered the ground. And then we realised that there was someone with us that we didn't know. He was just a kid, a few years younger than us. Funny though. We were drunk and kind of rambling but I'm not sure he was and he'd come out with this stuff that made us all laugh. And then all of a sudden he stood up and said, "Got to go". And he just took a running jump off the roof through the fog and onto the ground. He seemed to roll forward and onto his feet in one fluid movement and then ran off and out of sight. I'm pretty sure that was Patrick although I've never asked him. There are always too many other things to talk about, or not talk about, if you see what I mean.

Mostly, I keep trying to get him to write. He's full of so many ideas that are silly and surreal and ridiculous and they just make me crease up. Not using them would be a waste and I think he deserves a bit more than just doing manual labour. It's good pay but shit hours and hard going. The trouble is it's not easy to encourage someone to be creative when you're hardly following through on it yourself. Most of the time, all we end up doing is getting drunk and running about like idiots. I love it, I really do but we're kind of hurting ourselves. And I'm not sure how long we can keep doing this.

I'm suddenly feeling really tired and he looks like he's flagging too. We switch on the telly and then remember it's a Sunday morning so there's fuck all to watch.

"We could go to the Bell," he says to me.

"Yeah could do," I say.

I'm not keen and we've known each other long enough for him to recognise that.

"Nah, I think we both drank more than enough yesterday night."

"True," I say.

"I'm not sure I've been that pissed since London!"

He smiles at the thought and so do I. That was a hell of a time. Me, him and Tom spent three days at this hotel in Bayswater about a year ago. Our room basically looked like a crack den, despite a prominently displayed '*No Smoking*' sign on one of the walls. We were drunk when we arrived and it quickly degenerated from there. We managed to see three gigs in the three days and none of us can remember any of them very well. What is more memorable is the party in our room involving a dozen sixteen year old Swedish girls who were staying at the hotel; Patrick's claim that he was "Only drinking for the hangover"; meeting a Swedish couple on the last night who gave me some Snuff, me throwing up in the hotel stairwell after taking the Snuff; and the three of us trying to catch the train home, turning up two hours early and still missing it because we were all so wrecked.

For me though, the thing that sticks in my mind most is that when we'd gone there I'd always considered Patrick to be the mouthy one out of the two of us. I couldn't have been more wrong though. Unlike me, Patrick doesn't have to fill in all the silences that occur in a day. That much was clear by the end of our first day there, when I realised I hadn't actually stopped talking for about eight hours. It might be down to self-doubt. I usually don't know what to say or even how to feel, so I spew out words until I do.

That's probably why Patrick can tell that there's something on my mind now.

"Are you all right mate?" he asks, "Is Mary all right?"

"She was when I left hers at four this morning."

It sounds like bragging but that isn't how I mean it.

"You dirty dog," he says, with a laugh.

I was pretty sure that he'd come out with something like that. I still find it funny.

Neither of us speaks for a little while and I get the sense that he's thinking of something to say. Often, this is the prelude to some kind of elaborate or not so elaborate joke. Not this time though. He's actually quite serious:

"Are you thinking about your granddad?"

The question surprises me, even though it really shouldn't. Because that's the thing with Patrick and me. It isn't that we're incapable of being serious with each other, it's just that it doesn't always turn out the way you'd expect with most people. Quite often our conversations start sensibly until they veer off and we end up laughing at each other. This time is a bit different.

"Yeah, I am," I tell him.

I'm four years older than him, so that might be why I've never actually asked for his advice on anything major in my life. He's asked my advice on a few things before but all I ever did was confirm what he was already thinking. It's still not what we generally do, so I don't ask for any guidance this time either. He gives some anyway.

"I think you should go back and see your granddad. You'll regret it if you don't, Jon."

I know he's right too.

"I've never really lost anyone I was that close to," he tells me, "But if there was a chance that it might happen I'd definitely try to spend as much time with them as I could."

And then he shuts up for a bit. He's clearly said what he needed to say.

"If you want I can give you a lift to the hospital," he eventually adds.

I figure I should check in with Emily first. It still seems a bit early so I decide to have a cup of tea. Patrick has a coffee.

"What are you going to do today then?" I ask him.

"I don't know really. Don't expect there'll be too many people about."

"Lots of hangovers from last night, you reckon?"

"Maybe, but then again you don't look nearly as bad as I expected."

"Cheers."

He shrugs and grins at me.

"Stephen might be about, so I might go over and see him," he says.

We both look at the telly. 'Saturday Kitchen' is completely wasted on us. I'm not much of a cook and Patrick's managed to accidentally cook sausages on the 'broil' setting of his oven before. All the programme manages to do is make me bloody hungry.

"You hungry mate?" I ask, without looking away from the screen.

"Nah, Joe got up and made us some breakfast this morning. And he didn't even come close to burning the house down when he was doing it this time either."

I chuckle a bit at that and get up to go to the kitchen.

"I'm just gonna have a bite of something and then I think I'll give Emily a call."

The problem is that there's not a lot of food in the house. I really need to go shopping. Actually, I really need to do a lot of things. I should be cleaning or writing or sorting out the garden or doing some research. And I'm not doing any of those things. That annoys me but only because I know I'm probably not going to get the chance to do any of them today either. Too much is going on right now and I'd probably find a reason not to do them anyway.

I stick some bread in the toaster. It's my only option and at least I know there's some marmalade in one of the cupboards. While I wait for the bread to toast, I pace the kitchen floor torturing myself with what I could be doing and what I could've done this weekend if I hadn't wasted so much time enjoying myself. It's obviously pointless. I can't stop myself. I take a deep breath and it shuts off a bit in my head. There's still a feeling of unease and anxiety in the pit of my stomach though.

The toast is ready and I put butter and silver shred marmalade on it. I sit down next to Patrick on the sofa, eat the toast and start feeling a bit better. Then I go to the kitchen and put my plate into the slightly overfull sink. Another job to do, when I finally get round to it. I should probably have spent my advance on a dishwasher.

I get my mobile out of my jeans pocket and dial Emily's number.

She answers straight away.

"Hi Em. You okay?"

"I was just about to call you," she tells me.

"Why? What's happened?"

"Apparently, granddad's taken a turn for the worse."

"We need to get and see him then." I say straight away.

"That's exactly what I was going to say. The whole family needs to be there."

"Where's dad?" I ask

"I've been trying to get hold of him but I think his mobile's switched off."

"Well, keep trying," I say, "I'll make my own way and meet you at yours."

"Okay Jon. See you soon."

"Bye."

I walk back into the living room and sit down on the sofa next to Patrick. He doesn't look away from the telly, which he's turned over to the news. Just seems to be about a load of politicians talking.

"She all right?" he asks.

"Okay, I think."

I can't think of what else to tell him. It's not like it would change anything.

"Any chance you can give me that lift then?"

He turns his head and looks at me. I think he understands.

"Sure mate. When d'you want to go?" he asks.

"Pretty soon... She reckons his condition's got worse."

"Okay," he says, "I'm ready when you are."

That's when I hear three knocks on the front door. I get up and walk towards it. I look through the glass and I'm shocked by who I see. Standing on the doorstep staring back at me is my dad.

CHAPTER 23

David found it strange to be walking up the drive to the front door of his parent's old house. He'd gone to the bungalow without much thought and hadn't even called ahead to check it was all right with Jonathon; he could hardly be certain that his son wouldn't have done a runner if he had.

After getting back to the hotel the night before, he'd managed to sleep quite well. The bed had been comfortable and that, combined with overwhelming tiredness, had helped him drift off easily. Even so, he'd still only slept for about seven hours and, when he woke up he wasn't feeling particularly refreshed. He tried to get back to sleep. He didn't manage it.

There were too many things on his mind to make that possible. Some were completely beyond his control and he could accept that; although it hardly stopped him worrying about them. But the things that circled his brain most relentlessly that morning were definitely things he had the power to change.

Melissa had been right about him doing more for his kids. Letting life and the difficulty of where he happened to be living get in the way wasn't good enough. He thought about moving back to Norwich. That, though, still seemed a little premature. Things were still too awkward with Jonathon to seriously consider it.

He eventually got up, showered and dressed himself quite slowly. He put on white chinos and a red shirt and only briefly stopped to peer into the bathroom mirror. He looked okay; perhaps a little rough around the edges but not bad. By then, it was nearly eight o'clock in the morning and David still felt restless. After weighing up his rather limited options, he decided he would take a wander around Norwich to fill the few hours he had before meeting Emily and Melissa at the hospital.

The weather was pleasant that morning; blue sky, sunshine and enough of a breeze to refresh him as he walked away from the hotel. After cutting through the new bus station, he passed the old Norwich Union building; strolling along Theatre Street until a right turn took him past the clear glass crescent of The Forum building, which was the home of the public library.

David descended some steps and headed towards the market. Stepping slowly beside the bright and colourful stalls that covered the whole area, he realised he was passing the Sir Garnet Wolseley pub. He'd started going there when he was sixteen and was more-or-less a regular for another ten years after that.

He stopped and looked up at it, while standing in the shadow of the Church of St Peter Mancroft. It was closed but from the outside, the Sir Garnet looked like it hadn't changed much. David smiled when he thought back on what a great time he'd had and some of the stupid things he'd got up to; all the drinking, the arguments, the fights, the drink driving and the various close run things involving girls or police, or both.

There were no real details to his recollections anymore. Those were things that must have been lost years before. By then, it was more about the feelings than the facts, and he understood that sometimes the first thing on your mind can be the last thing you remember. His smile faded and he looked at his watch again. It was a quarter past eight and his mind had turned to Jonathon and his dad and to what Melissa had said to him about both of them.

David needed to stop wasting time. He knew that this might be his last chance to learn something more about his father before he was gone. He couldn't afford to keep making the same mistake he'd been making for most of his life.

He walked much more quickly going back. His lengthy stride taking him along Gentlemen's Walk and back onto Theatre Street. Within five minutes he was sitting in his car and putting on Radio 4.

David listened to a lot of talk about the 65th Anniversary of V.E Day, which he'd managed to forget had been the previous day. The big news about it was that the ceremony at the Cenotaph had been attended by all three party leaders because the Election result was still hanging in the balance. That, in turn, had led into another look at the 'extraordinary week in politics' that had just taken place; with a discussion about the ongoing talks between the parties, 'Coalition Politics', and about what it could all mean, or not mean and why everyone should or shouldn't care about any of it.

He switched it off after about five minutes and drove on in silence. Within half an hour he'd reached Harleston again, passing the recreation ground and the Swan Hotel before turning onto the Thoroughfare. With driving autopilot engaged again, he'd crossed Redenhall roundabout and then as the car reached the top of the hill, he'd stopped to look at the imperious old church that was to his right. It looked to him like nothing less than a perfect right angle made from flint, stone and glass; stretching up to caress the clear blue sky. Somehow it was even more impressive to him then than it had been when he was a kid.

The slow descent of just under a mile from Pear Tree Farm had taken him to his parent's home and he'd parked on the road outside the bungalow. A couple of dozen steps and three knocks on the front door brought him face-to-face with his son again.

Jonathon opened the door and looked at him.

"Hello Jonathon," David said.

It was only then that it fully registered to him just how nervous he was feeling.

"Hi."

"Sorry to just turn up like this. I wanted to see you."

There was a moment's pause, while Jonathon digested these words.

"Right then, you should probably come in."

David walked inside. He could hear the television was on in the living room around the corner. Jonathon closed the front door and then stood for a moment, quite close to David, hemmed in by the pale walls of the narrow hallway.

"Have you spoken to Emily?" Jonathon enquired.

"No, why? What's happened?"

"Apparently granddad's got worse. She thinks we should make our way to the hospital."

"Jesus! That doesn't sound good."

The worry and fear etched onto David's face was unmistakable.

"Do you want to sit down for a minute?" Jonathon asked.

"Yes. Thanks. Yes, I think so."

Jonathon quickly ushered David through the nearest door on the left of the hallway. Patrick Anders was sitting slouched on the sofa watching the news on television and he looked up at them as they walked in. David looked pale and strained and that immediately made Patrick sit up straight.

"Hi… Oh Jesus. You look terrible, Mr Gombrowicz!"

He switched off the TV with the remote control.

"Thanks Patrick," David said sarcastically, as he sat down next to him.

Patrick smiled.

"No, sorry. That's not really what I meant."

"I've just told him what Emily told me," Jonathon explained to him.

"Oh right… Yeah, that's pretty bad shit…" he took a deep breath and stood up, apparently looking for some sort of escape route, "I'll tell you what, can I get you both a cup of tea or something?"

"Thanks mate," Jonathon said.

"Please," David added with a nod and the closest thing to a smile he could manage.

Patrick walked out through the door and Jonathon sat down on the sofa. David's face continued to betray his thoughts and feelings better than any words could. The ever-present prospect of grief doing its best to consume his heart.

Jonathon barely acknowledged this and tried to lighten the mood instead. He looked at his father and told him in hushed tones so Patrick wouldn't hear, "He's not really very good at dealing with things like this".

"He's normal then," David replied, flatly.

"He'll make the tea and then he'll probably go home."

"I could use that kind of option myself."

Jonathon looked away. Staring ahead as silence filled the room again and they waited for their tea. When it arrived it wasn't really worth the wait. Patrick wasn't a tea drinker so he'd never had to become any good at making it. The two of them thanked him anyway.

"I should probably be heading off," Patrick told them without sitting down again, "You don't need me getting in the way... This is the time for family, I guess."

Jonathon looked up at him and smiled kindly.

"Thanks mate."

"Yes. Thank you Patrick," David added.

Although, the tea had been largely awful, the sugar in it had, at least, made David feel a little bit calmer and more ready to deal with the news he'd just been given. And what that meant was that he was able to talk around it rather than about it.

"This place doesn't look that different to how it was when I was a boy," he said to Jonathon.

"Nanny and granddad didn't really like changing things, did they?"

"No, but I still thought you might have made things a bit more your own."

There was silence for a moment as Jonathon searched for the words to explain.

"I just don't think I'd feel right about doing anything too much to it."

"It's your home now."

"Not really. It still feels like its nanny and granddad's... It probably always will do."

David found he couldn't disagree.

"Even when I was a kid living here, it was always more their home than it ever was mine," he told Jonathon.

"Is that why you left the first chance you got?"

"No, I left because your granddad had this amazing way of getting under my skin and making me want to throttle him. He could be a thoroughly irritating git."

"I think I can understand that," Jonathon said.

His statement was so deadpan that it took David a few seconds to recognise that Jonathon was making fun of him. When he did, he was glad. At least it was better than anger and hatred. Smiling for an instant, he thought he saw the semblance of a smile on his son's face too. If he did, it didn't last long.

"We should probably get moving," Jonathon said bluntly, "I just have to clean my teeth and grab a coat."

He got up from the sofa and left the room. David stood up and started wandering. The house didn't smell the same anymore; the harsh, sweet smell of his parent's favourite Mayfair cigarettes was gone, replaced by a blandly pleasant air freshener. The furniture and the carpets were different too; obviously Melissa and Emily's influence.

He walked into the hall and then into the kitchen. There was a huge pile of washing up in the sink. It looked like it had been left for at least two or three days. David shook his head. It was almost the only thing that fit in with being the home of a single man in his twenties.

He turned around and went back into the hallway, with its pale, faded wallpaper. A left turn towards where the bedrooms were, showed that it was just as dark as it had always been; a natural consequence of a lack of windows and natural light. As Jonathon came out of the bathroom, the light inside followed him through the doorway. Looking up, he saw David and stopped.

"Sorry. Just having a bit of a nose around," David explained.

"That's all right," Jonathon replied.

He went on into the bedroom opposite the bathroom. David followed him to the doorway and looked inside.

"You know that this used to be my room?" he said to him.

Jonathon was sitting on the bed. The room was a mess and there was remarkably little about it that David recognised.

"Yeah, I know. And it was the room that me and Emily used to sleep in when we were little and we stayed with nanny and granddad... I think you probably told us this was your room back then."

Over twenty years had passed since the whole family had regularly come to stay at the house. It had been years since David had even thought about it but looking back on it then, he realised what a special and fortunate time it had been; to enjoy such bright summer days, surrounded by all of his family; playing football in the garden with the two children, while Melissa and his dad and mum had sat and watched. Lovely, calm, happy times and he'd almost forgotten about them.

"Yeah, I think I probably would have mentioned it," he said.

Jonathon put his shoes on and tied them up. Then he stood and grabbed a denim jacket from the back of the door.

"Right we'd better be off," he said.

David led the way and Jonathon followed along the hallway to the front door. They both went outside and Jonathon locked the door behind him. They walked side-by-side and got into David's car.

CHAPTER 24

Dad starts the car's engine and the radio comes on automatically, just some bloke banging on about something to do with politics. He turns it off. Not in the mood I guess.

So, I sit in his car and don't say a lot, other than to let him know we have to go to Emily's house first. It's a difficult situation and I'm still not sure how I should react to him. We're in a rush although it hardly feels like it. I wish I'd had a pee before we left. And maybe a bit more sleep.

He sits there staring out at the road as he drives, turning left then right onto the A143. It's a grey day and a film of fog is obscuring the flat, green bottom of the river valley. I wonder what he's thinking. He looked pretty rattled when I told him about granddad. I've never seen him like that before. I always think of him as this hard, cold bastard and, secretly, I sort of like thinking of him like that. At the minute I feel bad for him and I don't want to. I know how shit he must feel even if I do still kind of think he deserves it.

He takes a deep breath. Like he's mustering the courage to do or say something.

"Your mum was telling me about your writing."

That's not good. He's trying to have a normal conversation. I can't do any kind of normal conversation with him, especially if he's going to start it by mentioning my mother.

"Oh yeah," I say.

"It sounded interesting."

'Interesting!' Is that really the best you can do dad? Can't you try a bit fucking harder with the disapproval?

"She told me that you did some research into your granddad's life before he came to England."

"Yeah that's right."

I wait for a putdown or something similar. It doesn't come.

"It's something I've always been interested in too. I even tried to do a bit of research into it myself before he… Well…"

"Lost his marbles," I say.

He laughs at that.

"Yeah well, I was looking for a more delicate way to put it but I suppose that's it."

"And?"

"And nothing much really. Researching things has never been my strongest suit. I found out a few things but there were a hell of a lot of holes in whatever the story really was."

"That's understandable though isn't it? There are a lot of people who might know things but don't want to go back over what happened because they were such terrible times."

"Do you think that's what dad. I mean your granddad did?"

The fuckers got me and I suddenly can't stop my mouth. Bollocks!

"Probably," I say, "At least up to a point. Except you've got to remember that he wasn't the only one. It's basically a whole generation."

He sits and digests this for a few moments as he pushes the indicator down to turn left at the Ditchingham roundabout. We drive on and the conflicting parts of me hope it is and isn't the end of the conversation.

"I know it is a little odd in terms of the timing but I'd be interested in knowing what you managed to find out, Jon."

He glances over at me and I see in his eyes that he's completely serious and that this is something he genuinely needs to know. I find that I can't deny him that.

"I need to tell you something first," I say.

It was my turn to take a deep breath.

"A decent amount of this is first hand although there is a fair amount that's still guesswork... I even went out to Poland and visited the village where he was born in Upper Silesia. The thing that amazed me most was how close it was to Auschwitz. You could almost see the camp from the village... You can't help thinking that the knowledge of that being there must have been absolutely horrendous... But yeah, anyway, the thing is that a lot of the really verifiable stuff was what came straight from the horse's mouth."

He looks confused.

"Not from dad?"

"Yeah."

"But how?"

"It's hard to explain but after nanny died and he was still living at the house on his own, mum and me used to visit him quite a lot. We wanted to keep him company even though it was just awful seeing him drift away. Losing touch with reality..."

I see his face tense up. I recognise the guilt.

"There could be times when he was fairly lucid though and that was when things, stories came spilling out... Once I'd managed to kind of train my ear to what he was saying I found it easy enough to understand. It was weird though because sometimes it was a whole mixture of languages. English, Polish, even a bit of Latin from the Catholic Mass I think... It was all over the place and sometimes he barely even knew who he was... There was a hell of a lot of conflicting things and half remembered experiences. Most of them were completely at odds with what and who he thought he was then. It must have been pretty awful for him when you think about it in that way."

"Poor old sod," I hear dad say under his breath.

We pass the Hedenham Mermaid on our left and I see how different the dull, mossy green paintwork is to its previously fluorescent vibrancy. I don't stop talking though:

"What I could gather from all this was that he was trained as a baker in his village. Some people from there could even remember him because, even though he was quite young at the time, he was really good at it... And he said it was the best job he ever had."

"Most of the jobs he had over here were pretty tedious."

"He was a hard worker though, so he made the best of things."

"Absolutely."

That was clearly a memory that was strong for dad.

"Anyway, so when the German's invaded that was the end of that job and anything like a normal life for him in Poland. He was put to work..."

"As a slave for a German family."

"That's right. And then he eventually escaped into one of the forests in the west of the country. There are actually quite a few in that part of Poland, so it's difficult to tell exactly which one it was. He was there for quite a while though. We're definitely talking months rather than weeks.

"How did he survive?"

"Probably by living on raw potatoes."

"Bloody hell."

"Yeah I know, but that wasn't completely unheard of at the time. And that was where he met up with the resistance."

"The Polish Home Army?"

"Yes. Things were probably a little bit more comfortable for him then. Relatively speaking"

"Of course. That makes sense."

"He would've got a few more regular meals at least and the Polish civilians at the edges of the forests usually gave them what they could... He'd still have been in hiding though, like the rest of the Home Army. They weren't in a position to attack directly so they based their operations in the forests for safety."

"So he was a bit like Robin Hood?"

I'd actually thought that before. I don't tell him.

"You could say that I guess... It would have been hard just to stay alive then. And at some point around that time, or maybe even earlier, he would've found out that his oldest brother had been killed."

"That must've been terrible."

"I'm sure it was, but it was hardly a unique experience for the time. There would hardly have been anyone he knew who wouldn't have lost at least one member of their family."

"I suppose not," he says.

I pause and take another deep breath.

"The problem was that, from then, his story started getting a lot patchier and less easy to understand."

"What do you think happened?" he asks, still looking at the road although I can see he's really somewhere else entirely.

"I don't know. There seems to be some evidence suggesting he might have managed to get to Warsaw. I couldn't say whether he was alone or part of a group or even exactly what his purpose was in being there... It doesn't look like there were any family or personal ties to the city for him. Still, it was the Capital of the country, so it was an obvious focal point for any resistance to German occupation... By then, he would have been quite a hardened soldier and would have had a decent amount of experience in fighting the Germans... Any conflict or uprising by the Poles in Warsaw was always going to need a fair amount of expertise to go along with raw bravery and knowledge of the city itself. It made sense for them to have brought in some experienced soldiers before the call to arms... It was all coordinated with the..."

There's a brief flash of light and I realise where we are. Dad does too.

"Shit," he says, "Bloody speed cameras."

When you don't pay enough attention through Poringland that's what happens. He slows the car down pretty quickly.

"Idiot!" he says to himself.

"Sorry," I say.

"What for? It's my fault."

He's right, so I don't say much for a few moments as we trundle on through the village. We only pick up any kind of speed again when we reach the end of it.

"You were saying," he says.

"Oh right... Where was I?"

"It was... Coordinated?"

"Yes... It was all coordinated with the arrival of the Russians, the Soviets, on the edge of the city. The Poles were hoping that if they rose up against the German's they could capture a lot of the key areas and hold on till the Russians entered the city and helped them finish the job. Then they'd have been able to drive them out of the city together... Of course, it didn't quite work out like that... The uprising was successful to begin with, and the Poles had control of a lot of the city, and key strategic areas... The problem was that the Soviet advance stopped short of Warsaw. And they refused to give any kind of air support to the rising... The Poles in the city had to fight for sixty three days with almost no outside support. In the end their losses were too heavy to carry on and they had to surrender to the Nazi's... That's the point where I really ran out of information to go on. I still think there are a couple of different things that might have happened to granddad then. It could be that he was captured and sent to a prisoner of war camp or he might have simply blended into the civilian population with the aim of continuing the struggle later on. Although that never actually happened, obviously."

"How did he get to England?"

"That's the thing. I'm really not sure. I know that he got here in July 1945. That's the first record I could find of him on British soil. And he met nanny about a year later."

Dad filled in the blanks of a story I'm sure I've heard but don't quite remember.

"She was standing on a bridge and he came over and spoke to her in really badly broken English. She thought he was handsome and he told her she was beautiful. She was a bit embarrassed but she knew that was he was the man for her... She always liked telling me that story when I was little."

He doesn't say anything else to add to that, so I start talking again.

"Going back to Poland definitely wasn't an option after that... But nanny was the reason he always kept his faith. Despite everything he'd lost and been through, it had still taken him to her. And he saw that as an example of God's providence."

He looks away from the road for an instant to look at me.

"Did he tell you that?"

"No," I tell him honestly and he looks back at the road, as we head into Norwich itself, "He told mum."

He looks back again and I assume he's checking my face for a lie. It's the truth so he doesn't find one.

We drive slowly through the city's winding streets and towards Emily's flat on Magdalen Road. The only sound I hear is the purr of the engine and my own breathing. His mind is somewhere else, apparently trying to take in everything I've just told him. I know it's not all that much. It's definitely not enough for me anyway. Way too many holes in this story for it to hang together properly. I don't know. There's got to be another way to make it work.

We get to Emily's flat and park on the road outside. Dad doesn't get out of the car though. Instead, he just sits, staring out through the windscreen. I want to say something. I've no idea what, so I keep my mouth shut. Then he looks at me.

"Are you going to write that book?" he asks.

"I dunno yet," I tell him, and I think that's the most honest answer.

He takes another deep breath.

"I think that you should."

"Maybe."

"There are gaps but it is fiction. It doesn't have to be a hundred per cent accurate."

I understand what he's saying. The problem is in finding a way to make it work and to find some way to end it. It still feels like both are completely beyond me.

"Give it time and think about it Jon."

He takes his seatbelt off, opens the car door, and gets out. I do the same with more things going through my head than I know how to deal with. There's no peace in it; only various vague hopes, jumbled and confused and leading me nowhere I recognise.

CHAPTER 25

He knew he was flying and he knew he was doing it at an incredible speed. Karski was largely gone though. What remained was a weapon, a death machine under the complete control of the Sinistrians. There was no need to look to see how far above the ground he was. He looked anyway and saw the darkness and blue smoke that had become so familiar. The world far below appeared to be nothing more than an advanced network of railway lines, with trains billowing smoke from their chimneys and engines.

There was no slowing as he took in the sight of more smoke. This time it was from the cities, towns, and villages of Pileck that were all on fire; bombed and burned as they were caught up in the ongoing battle.

The Sinistrians believed that the creation of The Manterrosh was destined to be the decisive turning point of the war; giving them possession of a weapon that was supposed to change everything. It was certainly a gargantuan and formidable mess of man and machine. A creature built in the image of its creators, with vast, black tattooed wings, blonde hair and goat horns on its head.

Where it differed from the Sinistrians themselves was mainly in its size. The Manterrosh was over a hundred feet tall and actually had armed Sinistrian soldiers standing in metal pockets that were grafted onto its sides and shoulders; to be used as additional firepower when it began its horrific work.

Despite this, it still had the appearance of an organic being; with pink skin stretched tightly over its workings and the remainder of Karski's organs; its legs were covered with thick light brown hair, while its feet were cloven hooves. Even so, it was far more mechanical than anything else, although it was not machinery or mechanisms that powered it. That power came from what was left of the heart and mind of Karski.

That didn't mean he had any control over the creature. He could feel the presence of Doctor Eugenius Stark and the Sinistrian leader, Erom Babylon, inside his head; controlling him. The two puppet masters making The Manterrosh do whatever they wanted.

By then, Karski was already aware of their plans and what they would make him do. He tried to resist but it was no use. His failure seemed inevitable because his strength was already being channelled into the workings of The Manterrosh. It was too much for him to fight.

The machine slowly descended and Karski knew that this was to be the first test of its power. The nearer it got to the ground, the more he was able to recognise the fear in the eyes of the Pilecki when they saw the monster he had become. Every one of them was doomed and he knew he couldn't stop it.

Bullets rained down upon them but they weren't shots designed to kill. They were shots used to control and to push all the people together. Of course, there were some fatalities from stray bullets and they were the lucky ones. It was the scream of The Manterrosh, which doomed many hundreds more of them. Its jaws opened and the flying death machine glowed white, from within and all the way out. Its banshee scream tore through the sky and the Amnios; ripping through flesh and bone to steal the soul of every single body that was in its path.

The excruciating pain of each and every one of them was absorbed in an instant by Karski's heart and mind. A feeling worse than death itself. An utter emptiness that only took away another part of him; the part of him that not even Doctor Stark had been able to touch and taint.

This was the real torture he was meant to endure. Every soul he would be forced to destroy would erode his own. More and more of his humanity would be lost until, eventually, there would be nothing left except the hollow shell of a soulless machine.

The Manterrosh flew on, levelling and emptying the towns and villages of Pileck with its deadly scream. Each time there was a single instant of terror and pain that was magnified a thousand times within Karski. And each time he recovered, weaker but still there, still alive inside a monster that he couldn't control.

He prayed for some kind of escape but it seemed to be impossible. Every time the machine flew up and away from Pileck, he felt some hope that no more innocent people would be killed. That hope never lasted long; The Manterrosh flapped its wings faster and swept down to destroy every Pilecki town and village on the road to Vistula.

Moving through the sky, the lights of the city appeared before him and once again, Karski tried to focus what strength he had on stopping the monster. It didn't work. It didn't even manage to slow it down. All it did was cause him more pain and made his mind drift away to another place entirely.

That was a relief in itself. For the first time, he felt calm and detached from the machine that was surrounding and engulfing him. He saw the sunlight of a summer day in his mind, as he watched himself walking towards a bridge. There was a beautiful girl standing on it with one of her friends. The girl had lovely long dark hair and she was wearing a red dress with a white flower pattern on it. He saw himself go and speak to her. He couldn't hear anything that he said though. Instead, he concentrated on her scarlet lips as they formed into a smile and her pale cheeks flushed red on her face. Then the girl's friend pulled her away from him and to the other side of the bridge. Karski stood and watched as she was taken away from him.

The vision in his head slowly faded from sunlight back into deeper blue and he saw that he had almost reached Vistula. He knew the plan was not to attack the city straight away. That was to happen later. There was a more important annihilation that was supposed to happen first. The Manterrosh was there to destroy the massed ranks of the Curzonian Army on the far side of the city. Erom Babylon had decided that this was the day, and the battle, that would effectively bring an end to the war.

Even though he'd seen it before, the sheer size and scale of the Curzonian Army was still a shock to Karski. There were at least half a million soldiers in human form, with nearly twice as many spiders. They all looked ready for battle; prepared to fight and, if necessary, to die in the name of their leader, Necrosarea.

As they moved into range, the Sinistrians that were in The Manterrosh's sides and shoulders began firing their machine guns. The Curzonians stood their ground, refusing to break from their formation lines. These weren't frightened civilians, they were soldiers and they weren't afraid to fire back at the vast, flying death machine. Their shots were accurate and the Sinistrians that had fired upon them only moments earlier were swiftly killed.

But bullets had nowhere near enough power to divert the machine from its path of destruction. It swooped down towards them and Karski knew what was coming. That didn't mean he could prepare himself for the sheer blinding horror of absorbing and crushing so many souls at once. In an instant, thousands were dead, and yet, The Manterrosh hardly made any dent in the Curzonian lines.

Karski found himself overpowered by the feeling of emptiness that followed. It also made him fully understand the desolation that surrounded the fire in the eyes of the Sinistrians. And he had to wonder then if he was gradually becoming one of them.

The creature circled and attacked again and again. More instant death followed. The killing was relentless and thousands upon thousands of Curzonians were simply annihilated. Many more still remained; all of them standing their ground and refusing to flinch, even in the face of such mindless, chaotic death.

The little that still remained of Karski was fading rapidly. His strength was leaving him and he could tell that he wouldn't be able to endure much more of this sustained torture. It was as if the icy fingers of death were reaching inside the workings of the machine towards him and there was no way to escape their touch; because the monster wouldn't stop, it would just keep on killing and sucking the life from him until he became just another of its victims.

And then he saw a figure, standing tall and powerful at the back of the Curzonian Army. Their leader, Necrosarea, was a vast and powerful man, easily matching the size, scale, and fearsomeness of The Manterrosh.

He was flying towards the great Curzonian and as he did so Necrosarea changed from a man into a huge and terrifying spider.

Before Doctor Stark and Erom Babylon could react, the spider had launched silk from the spinnerets on his abdomen towards The Manterrosh.

Karski could immediately tell that Necrosarea had found exactly what he was aiming for. The Manterrosh had been silenced. There would be no more deathly screaming because its jaws and throat were sealed by thick webbing that was stronger than steel. In his mind, Karski felt the panic of the Sinistrians and his relief at that made some of his strength return.

Necrosarea's next attack was even more sudden than the first. Springing up at the monster and biting with his venomous jaws, he managed to pierce the skin although there was little effect upon the machinery beneath. The Manterrosh managed to throw and then kick the spider away and onto the ground again.

With its vast wings flapping, The Manterrosh moved away, up into the sky. Without its deadly scream, it lacked the weapon to defeat Necrosarea. Doctor Stark knew this and wanted to retreat and regroup. This would have been sensible. Erom Babylon would not consent to it though. He refused to allow the Sinistrian's greatest and most fearsome creation to run away from any enemy, and especially not from a Curzonian. He made Stark turn The Manterrosh towards Necrosarea and attack.

In that single moment, the fight was lost. As soon as The Manterrosh started flying towards him, Necrosarea launched another attack. This time, he aimed his steel silk directly at the great black wings of the creature. Once again, his aim was extremely accurate. The Spinnerets of the great spider sent wave after wave of pale silk at the black wings; tying them down onto the body of the death machine so tightly that even their phenomenal strength wasn't enough to loosen the bonds.

At first it slowed the machine down, and then The Manterrosh was falling out of the sky, towards the ground. Necrosarea was there to help it on its way. The monstrous spider jumped onto it as it fell and, despite the kicks and punches aimed at him, he managed to bite into the machinery, just under the skin.

The effect was immediate. Karski felt a loosening of the Sinistrian's grip on his heart and mind. The closer he got to the solid, rocky ground, the more of his humanity returned. There was relief, or even pleasure, in that, although it couldn't stop the impact.

When the two creatures hit the ground, there was no soft, Deep Amnios to cushion them. There was only cold, hard rock. Necrosarea regained his human form to protect himself but the force of the fall was too much for The Manterrosh. It hit the ground and kept going, ripping through the rock that, in turn, ripped through the machine and tore massive pieces from it; flesh, blood and mechanisms all stripped away. And it kept on falling; growing smaller with every moment until there was almost nothing left. The Manterrosh came to its final stop on a ledge in a cavern far below the ground. And all that was left of it was the core of the body, mind, and spirit of Karski.

CHAPTER 26

Behind the green curtain, Stanislaw Gombrowicz remained unconscious, although his condition had stabilised. David was relieved but still wondered just how stable his father could actually be. The doctors had explained that he had an infection called Encephalitis and it was this, which had caused his collapse and coma. Apparently, some sort of relatively minor viral infection combined with his weakened immune system had led to the inflammation of his brain tissue. They made it clear that this, and his continuing deterioration, was ultimately down to his advanced age. David couldn't avoid thinking that his father's body was slowly shutting itself down.

He tried to stay positive anyway. Concentrating on the way the heart monitor was still constantly breaking the silence in the room and letting him know that his dad was still alive; still fighting in exactly the same way he'd always done. There was more reassurance in looking around and realising that, for the first time in many years, he was surrounded by his entire family. That couldn't be a bad thing, even if it was a shame that they hadn't assembled in better circumstances.

Sunlight was shining in through the pale curtains at the window and the room still seemed and felt grey; a veil of dark thoughts and feelings hung over all four of them and David couldn't stop himself thinking that it was little more than the deep breath before the inevitable plunge.

He tried turning his thoughts to the last time he, Melissa and both of the children had all been together. It was a struggle to recall and, when he did, he quickly remembered why it might have been better to forget.

They hadn't been in a room together since David's mum had died. The hospital ward that played out the final act of her life had seen a family both gathered and fragmented; with Jonathon and Melissa all but ignoring David, even as Emily was doing her best to remain neutral.

In the middle of all this, David had been forced to see just how frail his mum had become, as her heart had finally given out from the loss of her beloved Stan. She'd never really been the most formidable of women and, in the end, life had worn her down. Only five or six years earlier, she'd seemed relatively young but once Stan had been diagnosed with Alzheimer's the two of them were effectively racing to the grave. And she had ended up winning by a surprisingly large margin.

He sighed at that memory and Jonathon looked at him and then out of the window. David could tell that his son would rather have been almost anywhere other than where he was then. In a strange way, that made him feel proud that both of his children were strong enough to be there; facing death head-on in a way that he was sure would have been beyond him at their age.

He looked at his father again. Such a physically small man and such strength, of will, and of character. Then David glanced at Melissa and at the same time she looked back at him, holding his gaze for several seconds. There was a strange kind of relief in their shared look; and words suddenly sprang from David's mouth:

"Jonathon was filling me in on dad's life on the way here."

"Good... I think that it's something worth knowing."

"It's just a shame there are so many gaps in the story towards the end."

David looked over at Jonathon and said, "I actually meant to ask what you thought happened to your granddad after the Warsaw Rising. I mean, you told me there were a couple of possibilities..."

"Assuming he was there at all," added Emily.

"Of course... But if he was there, what might've happened and how did he manage to get over here?"

They all stared at Jonathon and he looked rather uncomfortable at suddenly being the main focus in the room. After a single deep breath, he started to speak, very slowly; deliberate and clear:

"Well, Emily and me have talked this through a few times and I'm still not completely sure what I think."

"All right then... What's the story you'd feel happiest to tell?"

Jonathon sat quietly for a moment and nobody else said a word.

"Okay then. I think... I think it's quite possible that he would have tried to blend into the civilian population after the Home Army surrendered to the Nazis in Warsaw. By then, anyone who did that would have known it was only a matter of time before the Soviets took control of the city. Most would have also assumed that not much good would come from that in the long term... The Russians were always going to go in claiming to be the liberators of the city... But the Poles weren't likely to believe that after they hadn't even given air support during the rising. Not to mention the centuries of rivalry and antagonism that already existed between the two peoples... I like the idea that granddad would have stuck around to help stabilise things in the city until the Russians launched their attack on the Germans... And that was when he got out... From there, it really is guesswork... But I've read a bit about these Polish Couriers that travelled between Poland and England to report to the Allies and the exiled Polish Government in London about what was happening ... It was seriously dangerous, flying in and out of the country. Making these incredibly long journeys, and by the end they'd usually be taking the worst and most dreadful news imaginable with them."

"Are you saying he could have been one of those Couriers then?" David asked.

"It'd be one way to explain how he got to England... Or maybe he knew a Courier, and they thought they could use whatever information he'd found out during the rising to pass on to the Allies. It's certainly an exciting story... On the other hand, it could be as simple as him travelling up the river to one of the northern sea ports, getting on a boat and sailing to somewhere like Sweden, before going on to England... That would've been quite difficult with all the ports under German or Soviet control and the country being in the grip of open war. Still, I guess it's no more difficult and it might be a bit more likely than him being a Courier."

He stopped for a moment.

"I haven't really answered your question have I?"

"You've answered it better than any of the rest of us could," Emily told him.

"We'll never know the whole truth," David added, "The good thing is that you know as much as you do. It means you can make an educated guess at the rest because it's something you care about... I only wish I'd felt the same way when I was your age."

David looked over at his dad and swallowed hard through the gathering lump in his throat. He stood up. His heart was feeling heavy.

"Excuse me," he said and walked beyond the curtain and then out of the room, shutting the door behind him.

He went out into the corridor and started to cry. There was pain running through his insides as he leaned back against the wall. An ocean of regret dragging him down and doubling him over.

"Dad," Emily said, as she walked out of the room.

Standing up straight against the wall, he looked at her. She went over and put her arms around him, saying nothing as she began to cry too.

David wiped his eyes and they looked at each other for a few moments without speaking. With a nod of his head, he took a deep breath and they both walked back through the door and into the room.

Jonathon and Melissa could see they'd been crying. Melissa stood up and Emily went over to give her a hug. Jonathon stayed in his chair, looking up at his dad. The concern on his face was obvious.

"Are you all right dad?" he asked.

"I'll be fine," David told him, without quite meeting his gaze.

They all sat down again. Emily and Melissa continued to dab their eyes with tissues that Melissa had taken from her soft, brown leather handbag. She offered one to David. He politely declined it.

They sat in a line beside Stanislaw Gombrowicz's bed, with David at one end and Jonathon at the other. Emily offered her hand to her dad and within seconds they were all linked together; sitting in silence. Ready and waiting for whatever was next.

CHAPTER 27

I'm not sure how long we've been sitting quietly like this. It might have been minutes or hours. What I know is that I really need to take a piss. It seems like kind of a big family moment though, so I don't want to ruin it. We're all here together and we're kind of all getting on. Granted we're all pretty miserable but even that's kind of a positive for us.

I've never seen dad like this before. I haven't always liked the guy but he was always my dad and he always seemed like nothing could hurt him. Even when nanny died, he seemed like he could tough it out. This time I'm not so sure. I'm worried about him and I still don't want to be.

I'm feeling quite uncomfortable. Not only do I need the toilet but my arse has now gone to sleep. Bloody chairs in these places always seem to be too hard. I have to say something. I need to get out of this room. I need some fresh air for a bit. I need to see what the time is. And, oh God, I need to find out if Mary's called me, my phone's still stuck on silent.

I stay where I am and don't say a word. Just thinking about anything other than granddad and my family makes me feel bad; must be Catholic guilt, even if it is two generations removed.

"I need a bit of air," Emily says, "I should call Oliver and let him know what's going on."

"Yeah I could use some air too," I say.

We step beyond the deep green curtain we're using to cut ourselves off from the others in the ward and we walk out together. She goes outside while I go to the toilet. I soon feel a hell of a lot calmer. I look at my phone. It's half four in the afternoon and she hasn't called me yet. Disappointed, I wonder what she's doing and immediately guess that she must be regretting everything that happened last night. I wash my hands and I regret it all too.

I wish I was stronger, and then I might be able to turn her down or let her go. It's not doing either of us any good. I can't help myself though, I've always wanted her. It's such a shame I'm not five years younger or she's not five years older. It would've been great to grow up with her in my life because really, she's just about my best friend. And right now, I'm genuinely thinking that if I can't make it work with her then I really won't be able to make it work with anyone.

I wash my hands and leave but I'm not ready to go back in and see granddad just yet. I go outside instead. Emily's still out there, so I stand around for a bit and, without actually listening, I hear her talking to her boyfriend. Sounds like it's made her feel better. And that's probably only because she doesn't have to pretend she's all right with everything.

She hangs up and I look over at her.

"Is he all right?" I ask.

"Yeah, he just wishes he could do more to help."

It's sweet. He's a good guy and that makes a change for my sister. I actually hope it lasts.

I put my phone on vibrate and hope for the best. Maybe Mary's out of credit or something. It wouldn't be the first time. She's been known to forget for days. Just long enough to get me worried until she texts to let me know everything's okay.

Or it could just be that she's doing something with her family. They do a lot together. They aren't like my family. There's nowhere near as much drama and you could never doubt that they absolutely love each other.

Maz and her sister, Laura, do wind each other up and I know they've said some pretty horrible things to each other in the past. Really, it's just that they want to be more like each other and, eventually, they're probably going to love that they aren't the same.

Her parents are awesome people too, and so forgiving and sweet. They don't judge Maz for anything. They let her live her own life. That's exactly how I think it should be. And she told me once that her mum liked that we were friends. Apparently, she trusts me, for some reason.

My phone vibrates in my pocket. I get it out quickly and look at it.

Patrick: *"You all right?"*

He's never been a man for using six words in his texts when one will do. This time I match him:

"Okay I guess."

I put the phone back in my pocket.

"Do you want to go back in now?" Emily asks me.

I don't know what to say so I decide to just be honest:

"Not really. I'm sort of dreading it."

"Me too," she says, "The best thing we can do is try and be there for dad."

"Yeah, I think you're right. There's not a lot we can do for granddad now."

"I just hope he isn't in any pain."

Nodding my head, I find I'm also hoping that dad isn't in too much pain about this either. I can barely believe I'm thinking that now. I guess it means I'm not quite as mad at him as I thought I was.

"Let's go in," she says.

Big sister taking the lead as usual. I've always preferred it that way and we can't stay out here forever.

The sun's still not made an appearance in the sky as I follow my sister inside. We walk along the corridor and back into the ward, which seems to be shaded pale blue by the small amount of light that shines in through the blue curtains at the window. Cut-off inside my family's green cocoon, mum and dad have moved to sit next to each other, so Emily sits down next to mum and I sit next to him. I look at granddad again and try not to let my thoughts go back to Mary.

My mind goes round whether the things I've assumed about what happened to granddad in Poland are actually true. Is there any other way he could have got to England? It's really is a shame that the records of these things are so vague. Or maybe not. I don't know right now.

If I could go out to Poland again it might help. Actually, we could all go. It'd be a good excuse for me, dad and Emily to have a look at that part of our family's history. Even if we didn't find out anything else about granddad it'd still be worth it.

"I think we should go to Poland," I eventually say.

I look at my dad, who says nothing for a moment and then slowly nods his head:

"Yes, I think that would be a good thing to do."

"Yes," Emily agrees.

Mum nods her head too and asks, "Are you going to write that book then?"

"I think I am writing it... Sort of, anyway..."

Then dad says, "The main thing is that you make a start, I'm sure you'll work out the rest of it in the end".

He's right, and that's probably the best advice he's ever given me.

I nod and half-smile at him as I lean back in my chair. Some of what has been weighing me down lifts but only briefly. I think about the room I'm in again and shuffle in my uncomfortable seat. The heart monitor and the other machinery attached to granddad's body keep doing their work and the four of us barely move.

Dad sits a little further forward, nearer the bed, leaning in and holding granddad's limp hand. He's managing to keep it together. There are no tears anymore, although I can see they aren't far from the surface.

It's the same for me except it's slightly easier to hold them in. I still wish I'd appreciated my granddad more before he got ill. I was an idiot then. I probably still am actually but at least I can see that now. He wasn't all fluffy like nanny was when I was a kid. She was a sweet lovely lady and he always had a bit of an edge to him. Not in a bad way, just not in a way that was easy to deal with. I still loved him though. He was my granddad and he was a kind man who loved me and Emily. Mum always knew that and I suppose that's why she's here now.

I suddenly feel strangely clear. My eyes are wide open and I can see that misunderstanding is one of the worst things in the world. I know how dad and granddad had some issues and they seem to have been these silly, simple, personal things based on not understanding, or not being willing to understand, each other. And it seems to me that things like that will only tend to distort and twist the love we have and make it into something negative; into something ugly and untrue. It's nothing but a waste of time. A waste of life. A waste of love itself.

That's not for me. I feel my phone vibrate in my pocket and wonder if it's Mary. I don't get time to look. Emily's seen something.

"Look," she says and points to granddad.

His eyes have opened. We all stand, gathered round the bed except for mum, who dashes out of the room to call a nurse. It's a shocking and wonderful sight. I quickly understand it. The old warrior is rousing himself for one last look at the world he's leaving behind. The sun shines into the ward through both sets of curtains and I see the light.

CHAPTER 28

He wasn't sure if he was alive or if he was only breathing. He was certainly free of The Manterrosh and that was something to be thankful for. Everything non-organic that had been grafted onto his body was gone and the terrible injuries from the surgery seemed to have been healed by the Amnios. Slowly, he opened his eyes to find that he was lying on a large grey stone ledge in an underground cavern, far below Vistula.

He was fully clothed in grey suit trousers and a white shirt. He stood and walked to the edge of the ledge. Below him was a vast expanse of darkness that seemed to have no end; an emptiness that went all the way to the very centre of the world.

Karski stepped away from the edge and looked back. There was a large hole in the rock above him. It was the hole he'd just fallen through, and the only way back to the city and the war that was still raging above him. He didn't make any move towards it. Instead, he looked and saw that Necrosarea, in his human form, was standing on the ledge, leaning against the rock face behind it.

"Hello Karski," he said to him.

He was smaller than before and the Curzonian leader looked remarkably ordinary, with his thick black hair and bushy moustache. Even so, dressed in a full khaki suit and tie, he was still every inch a military leader.

"Hello," Karski said.

"You're quite a beast."

"So are you," Karski replied.

"Indeed."

Necrosarea smiled at him and it looked like he was baring his teeth. He was certainly intimidating but Karski displayed no weakness.

"I should probably thank you," he told him.

"Yes, you probably could although you probably shouldn't," the Curzonian replied.

"And why's that?"

"Because I'm not finished yet."

"So you're going to kill me?"

"Oh no, I don't think so. I'm here to help you. Although you might not agree with me."

"Really?"

Karski knew better than to trust the leader of the shape shifters. He remembered what Witold had said about Necrosarea and what he had already seen in his own mind. That didn't mean he wasn't interested in finding out what he was planning and how he would go about his manipulations.

"What did you have in mind Necrosarea?"

His question seemed to come as a surprise.

"It's interesting. You don't seem scared of me."

"Why should I be?"

"You are bold. Or perhaps you are much more stupid than I thought."

"You still haven't answered my question." Karski told him, sharply.

Necrosarea would not be rushed. He walked towards him. Karski stayed where he was, although he did keep a wary eye on him. He wouldn't allow himself to be caught off-guard by any kind of attack.

But Necrosarea didn't even look at him. Going instead to the edge of the stone ledge, he sat down to dangle his legs over the abyss. He looked down into the darkness and spoke. His voice was calm and had an almost soothing tone:

"I wish to make you an offer Karski. You are a truly remarkable man although you remain oblivious to your true importance and potential... After all, you have already become The Manterrosh."

"I was made into it and you destroyed it."

"Of course that's right. What you do not know is that you can still become something greater and even more powerful than that creature... There is a prophecy, unknown to anyone but myself, that talks of a God named Vertaxos that will be created from a man who is born a Pilecki. You are that man Karski. If you allow yourself to become Vertaxos you will have the power to save your people. It is the only power that still can."

"And why are you telling me this?"

"Because I want you on my side. I need you to help me win this war."

Karski found this hard to believe. The incredible power and strength Necrosarea had already displayed was clearly far beyond anything the Sinistrians possessed.

"I think you're lying," Karski told him.

"I can understand that," he said, "It is quite natural for a Pilecki not to trust me. Natural and also very sensible."

Karski felt a pain in his side. A dull pain that he realised had been growing since he had woken up in the cavern.

"You have two choices," Necrosarea continued, "You can become Vertaxos or I can simply watch you die like the rest of your wretched people... There is only one sensible choice you can make. Become what you were born to be and save your people... The man you are, were, and can still be will be gone and forgotten if you do not become Vertaxos."

His voice remained gentle and calm, even as his threats became more obvious. More than that, the pain in Karski's side was getting worse and he was suddenly aware that he was dying. He stumbled a little, as he tried to move.

"My poison works quite slowly, so you have lots of time to make your decision. But, needless to say, the sooner you make it the less pain you will have to endure."

Karski looked down at the right side of his torso and saw that his shirt was bloodied in the pattern of a huge spider's fangs. He sat down on the stone ledge as the blood on his shirt started spreading as swiftly as the poison was spreading through his body.

As he weakened, he started to hallucinate; and that, in turn, revealed a side-effect to the poison that Necrosarea could not have expected. The potency of the venom amplified his visions, making them clearer and more vivid than they had ever been before.

The first thing he saw was the total destruction of Vistula that was taking place above him. It looked like a plague of giant spiders imprisoning the Pilecki within their webs while, at the same time, buildings were demolished and pulled down. The art and culture of the Pilecki wiped out by the force and relentless power of the Curzonians. The spirit of Karski's people crushed by Necrosarea's power and betrayal.

It was enough to show Karski that Necrosarea might have been honest about what would happen if he didn't join with him. But that still wasn't enough to make him give in to the great Curzonian's demands. He couldn't shake the feeling that it was just as likely that the betrayal of the Pilecki and the outcome of the war were inevitable no matter what he did.

His mind looped around an idea, the single thought that Necrosarea was actually trying to stop him from doing something; forcing his hand by poisoning him to prevent him doing what he was supposed to do. There was a strange desperation in his actions and Karski refused to give in until he knew the reason for it.

Another vision appeared. It was a beautiful sunny day somewhere far away from the land of Pileck. He saw himself outside a church. He looked happy. There was a woman in a long white dress on his arm and she was smiling too. He recognised her. He recognised the long dark hair, the pale skin and the red lipstick. She was his wife. A wife he hadn't met. She was beautiful and he loved her. He knew that he always would. He remembered her name was Anne.

Then she was gone and he saw a boy in dungarees instead; blonde haired, blue eyed and playing football in the garden of what would one day be his home. The boy looked happy and then he saw himself there too; older and with his hairline in retreat and greying. There were more lines on his face but he saw pride in being with his boy; with his son, with David.

Fading away and back towards darkness, he saw Witold. His friend looked battered, thin and exhausted but he was safely aboard his plane taking him back to the Alliance. There was hope for the Pilecki. He trusted his friend's belief on that. There was relief in the realisation, even though the situation was still desperate.

That was when he saw what Necrosarea was trying to do. The betrayal of the Pilecki was already happening and he couldn't change that. Necrosarea was actually trying to keep him from another life. His real life, with a wife and a family of his own and the chance of happiness away from the war.

"Per Omnia saecula saeculorum."

He heard the words in his head and this time he understood what they meant to him. He opened his eyes slowly and was still where he had laid himself down on the ledge. Necrosarea was standing above him, his face impassive and intimidating.

By then Karski's shirt was almost completely soaked with blood and the pain in his side grew worse with every moment. It was an awful dull and tortuous feeling that affected his entire body; far worse than the burning pain of Eugenius Stark's brutal modifications and closer to the pain he felt inside The Manterrosh; except that it was somehow even more malevolent; more hateful and lingering; and not at all empty. Instead, it was filled almost to bursting point with evil that toyed with his body; the pain being magnified further by brief periods of release that were swiftly followed by an intensification of his agony, repeated over and over again.

"You're back Karski," Necrosarea said to him.

"It certainly feels that way," Karski replied, trying to sit up.

He winced as he did so.

"Is it very painful?" the Curzonian asked him.

"Quite," he lied.

"Interesting. I've always wondered what it must be like to be weighed down by the poison of a superior civilization. It must be a fascinating experience for you."

"It must be."

"Have you made your decision yet?"

"I will not betray my people."

"Then you will do as I have said?"

"That isn't what I meant."

"But that can be your only meaning. You must become Vertaxos to save your people."

"Really? Then would you please explain to me what you would gain from me doing that."

"Aha very good. You do have some intelligence then Karski... I need you to help me gain complete control over the Sinistrians and the Alliance. The two of us together are undefeatable. And I would even be so good as to allow you to save your people."

"And I would be under your control too."

"Naturally. I would be the one who made you. Don't worry though, there are a great many benefits to being the closest ally to a living God."

Karski slowly tried to get up. The pain was excruciating. Necrosarea only watched him, apparently enjoying Karski's discomfort. He eventually managed to stand up straight.

"I think you may be lying about how much pain I am causing you," the Curzonian leader told him.

"And I think you might be lying to me about everything else."

Necrosarea gave his horrible, teeth baring smile again and Karski's pain intensified.

"No my friend. I am sorry to have to tell you that the choices I have offered are all that you have."

"So, I can stay here as your slave and never see my family again or I can leave my people to death and defeat?"

"That's right Karski. That's exactly right. Well done for figuring that out. After all, I have only told you this several times already... Although, to be fair, I do appreciate that you are in rather a lot of pain."

Karski stood next to Necrosarea. In this form, he was a little taller than him, despite being hunched over slightly by the pain.

"It's not much of a choice."

"Yes," Necrosarea said, flatly, "You're right of course. But perhaps you should look at it as less a matter of choice and more about deciding on what you really want to believe."

There was no decision for him to make. Despite the pain, Karski already knew what he believed. He had faith and love for the Pilecki and for people like Witold. Or anyone brave enough to lay down their lives or endure all kinds of hell for their people and their country. He was sure that they were the people who would save Pileck and each other. He was equally sure that it was not a job he was up to.

There was only one solution. He had to leave because he believed in something different; he believed completely and utterly in love. He looked at Necrosarea and held out a hand to him. The Curzonian took hold of it and Karski spoke into his face:

"I know what I believe in and I don't believe in you."

He took hold of the shape shifter and dragged him over the side of the ledge and down into the abyss. As they both fell, Karski managed to summon up all his strength to punch Necrosarea in the face. It was enough to stun him and stop him returning to his spider form to save himself.

Karski looked down through the empty darkness at a dot of light appearing distantly below him. The light grew bigger and brighter in his eyes and he realised that Necrosarea was gone. He didn't know where and he didn't feel like it mattered much anymore. He was heading home.

The light grew brighter in his eyes as he saw the vision of David and his grandchildren, Emily and Jonathon, playing in the garden of his home in Wortwell. He and Anne were sitting, hand-in-hand, watching them happily. His heart felt full of love and he knew he had made the right decision.

Every moment of his life as Stanislaw Gombrowicz, in England after the war, returned to him as he continued to fall towards the light. It had not always been perfect but it was the life he had chosen; with the family that divine providence had given him and it was this that was his true saving grace.

He closed his eyes to the empty later years and, when he opened them again, he saw David, Emily and Jonathon standing at the bottom of a bed looking at him. He felt their love and knew that was all he had ever needed.

'*Sky of blackness and sorrow (a dream of life)*
Sky of love, sky of tears (a dream of life)
Sky of glory and sadness (a dream of life)
Sky of mercy, sky of fear (a dream of life)
Sky of memory and shadow (a dream of life)
Your burnin' wind fills my arms tonight
Sky of longing and emptiness (a dream of life)
Sky of fullness, sky of blessed life (a dream of life)'

"The Rising"
Bruce Springsteen

ABOUT THE AUTHOR

A writer of multiple genres, James Eddy began writing film and television scripts before moving into Short Stories, Novels and Novellas. The Dark Era is his debut novel. For more information, please   visit   www.jameseddy.co,.uk or feel free to contact him via <u>Twitter</u> or <u>Facebook.</u>

ABOUT YOUNGBLOOD BOOKS

Founded in 2012, Youngblood Books is owned and operated by James Eddy. We publish, and plan to publish, a diverse range of genres, including Comedy, Drama, Children's Stories, Romance, Fantasy, Literary Fiction and Comics. Visit us at <u>www.youngbloodbooks.co.uk</u> to keep up to date with all our new releases.

Please feel free to leave a review wherever you may have purchased this book from. Many thanks.